HARRY
The Legacy of Harry Enstrom

Harry Enstrom, an adventurous boy of fourteen years old, left home early one morning, and enrolled as a deck boy at the Shipping Office in Landskrona, Sweden. He would bravely roam the deep and dangerous seas of the Antarctic, the Pacific and Indian Oceans during the whale catching era.

Arriving in South Africa he packed his bags and left the boat. He ultimately enlisted in the Anglo Boer War in October 1899, as Trooper 289, Bethunes Mounted Infantry.

Harry was involved in the skirmish which took place at Scheeper's Nek near Vryheid, on May 20, 1900. As he lay injured in the dust, he experienced the mayhem and confusion. The orange flashes of Mauser fire and the whizzing and whining of bullets ricocheting all around him, listening to the screams and yells of fellow troopers. He was subsequently taken Prisoner of War.

The Pioneer of the Enstrom family in South Africa lived his life dangerously and to the fullest. The war had left him a legacy of pain, suffering and sacrifice. To his family he left a legacy of bravery, fearlessness, and valor.

Seventy years later his Grandson, Aubrey, left the shores of South Africa. As the ship sailed from Durban harbour, the Bluff, where Harry had settled, loomed in the background.

The Pioneer of the family in Australia would experience the adventurous life which his Grandfather had longed for. He would enjoy the opportunities and freedom; live on board a forty-foot yacht for five years cruising the east coast of Australia, everything which his beloved grandfather had yearned for.

As his Grandfather before him, Aubrey would ultimately succumb to heart failure. He too would leave a legacy of moral integrity, courage, and heroism.

This book is dedicated to the Ancestors,

and Descendants of

Bror Emil Hjalmar Enstrom

Pioneer of the Enstrom Family in South Africa

And

Aubrey Allen Enstrom

Pioneer of the Enstrom Family in Australia

HARRY
The Legacy of Harry

Written by

Rosalie Angeline Moore Enstrom
Author and Family Historian

Rosalie – traditional and classic.

The bird is powered by its own life and by its motivation. A.P.J. Abdul Kalam

Other Works by the Author

My Memoirs of our Fifty Golden Years

Stockholm to Durban

The Osmers' Family History

Flight to Freedom

The Silent Knight and other Short Stories

Longlist Winner of Sydney Hammond Memorial Short Story Writing Competition 2019

Entries in the Caboolture Writer's Link Anthology 2020

This is a book of fiction. All the information in this book has been collected, researched, and written with love and respect for all those who have gone before us. Love and respect too for those of our family who are still living as they too will one day become history. Events are based on facts which are a compilation of my research and interpretations. These have been carried out over a period of over twenty years, coupled with the stories and contributions of family, alive or now dead.

This book has been written through the unconditional love that I have for my Late Husband, Aubrey Allen Enstrom, his Brother Wallace Stanley Enstrom, his Father Wallace Vivian Enstrom and his Grandfather, Bror Emil Hjalmar Enstrom (also known as Harry, whom I never had the pleasure of meeting).

I also want my children to know that they were part of a long chain of people spreading wide and deep into the past and that they have some responsibility for expanding it into the future. They have been left a legacy of bravery, fearlessness, and valour; and it is hoped that they will use it.

I have endeavoured to provide all references, however, my sincere apologies for any source or reference which has been missed or overlooked. Any errors or omissions were definitely not intentional.

My Very Special Thanks

Aubrey Allen Enstrom
My Beloved Late Husband
8 Jan 1937 – 7 June 2018

For all the love and protection which he provided for me
And our family over the years.

Rowena Wattrus
Who painstakingly emailed to me all the copies of the medical
records which she sourced and photographed from the Kew
Archives in London.

Joan Hope
For the use of the history of the Ziervogel Family

Johan van Breda
For the documentation and photos of the van Breda Family

Phyllis Enstrom (Decd)
Who provided the photographs of our Ancestors

Rosemary and Tempest Enstrom
Who provided the newspaper cutting to the "Rate Payer" by
Lenard Enstrom

Carl and Debbie Boock
For the contribution of photos and information

The South African Defence Force
For providing copies of records in respect of:
Lenard Enstrom
Erik Stanley Enstrom
Wallace Vivian Enstrom
John Harold Enstrom
James Moore
Joseph James Moore
John Charles Moore

The South African Military History Society
For permission to use information and photos.

My Children
Jennifer Rose Enstrom (Deceased)
Gary Patrick Enstrom
Mark Aubrey Enstrom
Kerry Leigh Enstrom
Susan Claire Enstrom Vidler

My Grandchildren and Great Grandchildren
For all the love and joy that they give.

Larry and Lana Wright
For the 41 years of friendship through the good times and the bad.

Wayne Brown
For his invaluable assistance as a Vietnam Medic in providing
information
As to what "Harry would actually have been through" when
wounded in action.

Russell Perry
My "Special Thanks" to Russell Perry who has provided valuable
assistance in the design of the cover.

Michael and Angela Claxton
My sincere thanks and appreciation for your valuable friendship
and support.

Epigraph

We shall defend our island,
Whatever the cost may be,
We shall fight on the beaches,
We shall fight on the landing grounds,
We shall fight in the fields and in the streets,
We shall fight in the hills;
We shall never surrender.

Winston Churchill

Map of Natal Battlefields

Courtesy: AngloBoerWar.com

Table of Contents

We are the Chosen

We are the chosen. My feeling is that in each family there is one who seems called to find the ancestors. To put flesh on their bones and make them live again. To tell the family story and to feel that somehow those who went before know and approve. To me doing genealogy is not a cold gathering of facts but, instead, breathing life into all who have gone before. We are the storytellers of the tribe. All tribes have one. We have been called as if it were in our genes. Those who have gone before, cry out to us: "Tell our story!". So, we do.

In finding them, we somehow find ourselves. How many graves have I stood before now and cried? I have lost count. How many times have I told my ancestors, "You have a wonderful family; you would be proud of us". How many times have I walked up to a grave and felt somehow there was love here for me? I cannot say.

It goes beyond just documenting the facts. It goes to who I am, and why I do the things that I do. It goes to seeing a cemetery about to be lost forever to weeds and indifference and saying, "I can't let this happen". The bones, here are bones of my bone and flesh of my flesh. It goes to doing something about it. It goes to pride in what our ancestors were able to accomplish. How they contributed to what we are today. It goes to respecting their hardships and losses, their never giving up, their resoluteness to go on and build a life to their family. It goes to a deep and immense understanding that they were doing it for us, that we might be born who we are, that we might remember. So, we do.

With love and caring and scribing each fact of their existence, because we are them and they are us. I tell the story of my family. It is up to that one called in the next generation to answer the call and take their place in the long line of family storytellers. That is why I do my family genealogy, and that is what calls those, young and old to step up and put flesh on the bones.

Author Unknown.

Courtesy: Johan van Breda.

Introduction

I arrived at Macleay Island on a tranquil sunny day in June 2005, and immediately sealed the deal. The peace, and serenity, was what I needed to write the family history. Writing and living in this environment not only allowed me to focus on my passion for sailing and the sea; this was where I would set up an office where I was able to spend hours writing the rich history of our forefathers. A journey which extended far beyond my wildest dreams. As I looked out of the windows and from the deck, I dreamed of the riches which had never been told. The seas which had been sailed, the wars which had been fought. There was time that no clock could measure for this was the realm of all my dreams.

I first became interested in the study of family history some twenty years ago when I set about trying to find the name of my husband's biological mother who was killed in an accident when he was only two. I thought how terrible it must have been for him never to have known anything about his mother, his grandparents or his extended family. It took several years before I made a breakthrough. Finally, the picture was almost complete as I wrote the book "Stockholm to Durban" which tells of a young man from Stockholm who sailed the oceans and the seas on whaling vessels. He eventually settled in Durban but not before taking part in the Boer War. This young man was my husband's grandfather, Bror Emil Hjalmar Enstrom. The family history also took into account the service of Jonas Qvist in the Napoleon War, Johan Enstrom, Harry's Grandfather and the service in World War II of the four sons of Harry Enstrom.

I cannot put over twenty years of research into a short story, but researching the history became so interesting – it was about our family ancestors who can directly be attributed for shaping the history of South Africa. What was of even more interest was the fact that my husband's ancestors had a direct link to the Osmers' Family, my maternal ancestors, in that Anna Suzanna Ziervogel (third Great Grandmother to my husband) was also the first cousin to Dietlof Siegfried Marè, Grandfather of Carolina Augusta van Heerden who was married to Johannes Alexander Osmers, my Grand Uncle.

Just as the history of the van Breda Family, dating back to the 1670's saw Aubrey's Sixth Great Grandfather, Pieter van Breda, who was born in the Netherlands in 1696, a soldier in the VOC (Vereenigde Nederlanden G'Octoijeerde Oostindische Compagnie aan Cabo de Goode Hoop, en resorten van dien), a farmer, while he plied his trade as a tailor and undertaker in the Cape, and who had a son also named Pieter van Breda. The younger Pieter became Captain in the Burgherwag, member of the Burger Senate and farmed on the farm Oranje Zigt.

This book, therefore, records the story of the life of Aubrey Allen Enstrom and that of his Grandfather Bror Emil Hjalmar Enstrom, (also known as Harry), both Pioneers in their own right.

Researching and writing the family history provided so much insight into the lives of our forefathers. There were those who were ordinary simple living people, working as farm labourers, craftsmen, security officers, and participating in serving their respective countries in war. On the other hand, there were members of the van Breda Family who were slave owners and very dominant in land ownership mainly in the Cape. There is pride that the significant icon, the Agulhas Lighthouse on the southern tip of South Africa can be directly attributed to our great ancestor, Michiel van Breda. He had donated the land on which this stands. The Ziervogel Family too were very influential landowners, farmers, doctors, lawyers, and professors.

The story begins when Harry Enstrom migrated from Stockholm, the capital of Sweden to finally settle in Durban South Africa. Harry was an adventurous young boy when at the age of fourteen years, he enrolled as a deckhand on the whaling ships which were operating in that era. He would endure the hardships of life on the ocean and having had enough he jumped ship in South Africa and enlisted in the Anglo Boer War, only to be wounded in action at Scheeper's Nek and taken Prisoner of War.

Harry was undoubtedly the *pioneer* of the Enstrom Family in South Africa and according to our father, Wallace Vivian Enstrom, (also known as Wally), Aubrey and his family too were the *pioneers* of the family in Australia, after migrating in 1970 of which we are immensely proud.

The Bluff, Durban, where Harry settled is certainly not as it was in the late 1800's when he first entered the harbour and ultimately made South Africa his home. I have wondered and marvelled how the years have brought change. The South Africa where Harry Enstrom once settled has changed dramatically. The 1800's posed a challenge to colonists who colonized the country with determination and courage to build a country which would prove to be second to none. Those who migrated to South Africa ultimately migrated to find a better life and today, as in those days when migration was to South Africa, migration is from South Africa, once again for those descendants originating from our early forefathers trying to find a better life in other countries. Harry was looking for that better life; now his descendants are leaving South Africa for the same reasons, a better life and future for their families.

In the early 2000s Aubrey and I lived on Macleay Island, a unique little island in Moreton Bay, Queensland, Australia. Living on the Island, our lifestyle resembled the lifestyle which Aubrey and the other Enstroms enjoyed when living on the Bluff many years ago, where they were free to roam, fish and enjoy the beaches without any fear. Macleay Island was where we were able to watch our three grandchildren who were resident on the island lead a carefree lifestyle without all the fear and problems being experienced on the mainland. They were living very much the same as their Grandfather did, swimming, fishing and being carefree and it seemed as though time had come full circle.

Ancestral War Participation

An army marches on its stomach.
Napoleon Bonaparte

Jonas Milberg
Third Great Grandfather to Harry Enstrom

According to the Household Examinations Records Snuggarp, Jonas Milberg was recorded as a soldier. He married Karin Andersdotter (Skirö C:1 P159). They had unknown number of children, one of whom was Anders Jonasson who was born February 17, 1747 in Snuggarp, Skirö. He was named Anders from his Mother's surname and Jonasson, Jonas' son.

Anders Jonasson
Second Great Grandfather to Harry Enstrom

Anders Jonasson was born on February 17, 1747. He married Maria Johansdotter who was born in 1756 in Mugarp Margaretagard, and they had three children:

    I.   Catharina Anderson, born in 1774 and who died at the tender age of four years;

    II.   a second daughter also named Catharina Anderson was born in 1779; and

    III.   a son Jonas Anderson was born on May 23, 1785.

All the children were born in Skirö Parish.

The family moved to Klackenhult in Karltorp Parish in 1793 and Anders' occupation was listed in the Household Examinations Records as a farmhand. In Anders' instance it is not clear whether in fact he was a *"torpare"* (someone who was permitted to use a small part of the land of the property and live in the *torp* (cottage) or whether he was paid by living and working on the property, either way his conditions of service would not have been far from slavery.

Dragon Jonas Anderson (Qvist)
Great Grandfather to Harry Enstrom

Jonas Anderson was the son of Anders Jonasson and Maria Johansdotter. He was born on May 23, 1785 in Skirö Parish and died on April 22, 1863. On April 8, 1809 at the age of twenty- four years old, he married Helena Eriksdotter and they had five children:

I.   Anna born on August 25, 1810 and who died on November 11, 1810;

II.   Maria born on January 24, 1812;

III.   Johan born May 4, 1815. Johan died on May 28, 1935 from Tuberculosis;

IV.   Jonas born on June 24, 1819; and

V.   Greta Ann born July 5, 1822.

All the children were born in Karlstorp Jonkopings Parish. (Hagterpet Ekenäs Malilla).

According to the household record, his parents Anders and Maria who were poor, were living with him. His sister Catharina was extremely poor, handicapped and was ill.

Jona's mother, Helena Eriksdotter was born in Bondarp in Karlstorp's Parish on August 15, 1787. She was the daughter of farmer Erik Larsson Kullberg, born in Ökna Parish in Torpa on December 21, 1752 and Margareta Johansdotter, born 1759. Helena had two sisters, Annica born on March 22, 1783 and Maria born on November 23, 1791.

Sadly, Erik Kullberg was killed on May 26, 1810 by a fallen tree. Margareta Johansdotter died from Pneumonia on February 2, 1817.

Erik Kullberg was the son of farmer Lars Olofsson and Annika Larsdotter.

Harry's Great Grandfather, Jonas Anderson became Dragon Jonas Qvist, a soldier name, in 1805 in Klackenhult in the Napoleon War at the age of twenty years. According to Hans Hogman, he was Dragon No. 55 in Vetlanda Company and belonged to the Stora Röslida "rote". His soldier croft (Dragontorp) was in Skede Parish (Record from register 1812) His horse was a six-year-old yellow Vallack with white back feet. Jonas was twenty-eight years old.

Jonas Qvist had a patronymic name prior to his time as a soldier in 1805, and in this instance, it would have been Jonas Anderson. When he enlisted, he was given the soldier name "Qvist". It was not common for a soldier to keep his "soldier" name when he left the military and, normally, they readopted their previous patronymic name, however, during the last part of the nineteenth century a soldier normally kept his "soldier" name when he left the service.

The *Dragontorp,* was a cottage or croft wherein a *dragon* (dragoon) lived.

At the age of twenty-eight years, Jonas was deployed in the Napoleon War 1813 – 1814 in the so-called Northern Army led by the Swedish Crown Prince Karl Johan. King Karl Johan XIV was Commander-in-chief of the allied Northern Army which consisted of 155,000 troopers. The regiment was shipped to Germany in May 1813 and returned to Sweden in the spring of 1814. The actual battles in which they served on the continent are unknown, however, the 1814 Campaign was considered one of Napoleon's masterpieces as he faced the allied forces of Russia, Prussia, Austria and Sweden after suffering a devastating defeat in Russia.

The war was with France and Denmark and Swedish allies included England, Russia, Austria and the German States. The campaign in Germany was against Napoleon (France) and a war with Denmark who were allies of Napoleon. The results were peace on January 15, 1814 in Kiel with Denmark and on May 30, 1814 in Paris with France. Sweden being the victors. Jonas then returned home.

In the Peace Treaty of Kiel Denmark Norway was given up to Sweden. The Norwegians resisted, but the following year had to accept a union with Sweden, as a double monarchy. Both countries had separate laws, constitutions and governments, but the same head of state. (Swedish Roots).

Jonas belonged to the Småland Dragoon Regiment (*Småland Dragonregemente)* and it was interesting to research some of the regiment's history as the regiment changed its name, and in some degree equipment, arms and tactics at several times.

The regiment was first established in 1628 as the *Småland Horsemen (Smålands ryttare)* and was linked to the Allotment System in 1695. In 1684, the regiment received the name *Småland Cavalry Regiment (Smålands kavalleriregemente)* and in 1802, the *Småland Light Dragoon Regiment (Smålands lätta dragonregemente).* In 1808, the regiment received the name the *Småland Dragoon Regiment (Smålands dragonregemente).*

The regiment was divided into two units in 1812.

The former 2nd Battalion of the *Småland Dragoon Regiment (Smålands Dragonregementes infanteribataljon),* and the former 1st Battalion of the regiment kept the name *Småland Dragoon Regiment.* However, this name was changed to the *Småland Hussar Regiment (Smålands husarregemente)* in 1822.

The regiment was disestablished in 1927.

The brigade's history goes back to the *fanor* that was raised in the counties of Kalmar and Kronoberg (province of Småland) in 1543, and was allotted with 1000 *Rusthåll* hence the regiment had 1000 cavalrymen organised into eight companies; all were located within the province of Småland. After 1812 when the former cavalry battalion was divided, the new dragoon squadron had five hundred cavalrymen organised into six squadrons of eighty-three men each. Jonas was one of two hundred and fifty *rusthåll* who was located in the county of Jönköping; the county Kalmar one hundred and thirty-eight, and the county of Kronoberg one hundred and twelve.

The regiment was organised into five squadrons in 1833. Location of the primary Garrison of the Regiment: From 1906, Eksjö.

Jonas moved to Jareda Parish in 1815 when he left the army after ten years of service and then moved on to Marholma in Karlstorp in 1818.

The Allotment System, according to Hans Högman, was how the soldiers in the infantry and the navy personnel were recruited by a system called *utskrivning* whereby every fit man in villages and farms throughout the countryside were grouped together in a *rote* (ward). Each *rote* consisted of ten men between the ages of fifteen and forty. One man per *rote* was involuntarily recruited to serve in that *rote's* Regiment and it was thus that Jonas was conscripted. The towns and cities were not a part of the army recruiting system, but the navy recruited in towns and cities as well as in the countryside.

The cavalry did not use the system of choosing every tenth man like in the infantry. The cavalrymen were voluntarily recruited among men in villages and farms and normally it was the farmer himself who rode. The farmers who joined the cavalry got a tax deduction as a compensation. The recruiting requirements was decided by the government each time there was a need to mobilize the army. Normally, the veterans were recruited first. This system had many disadvantages as Generals never knew in advance how many soldiers they could recruit at each time, so they never really knew the strength of their forces in advance.

The system was also widely disliked by the farmers and their farmhands. At any time, a farmer or his hands could be designated the "tenth man" with no alternatives but to be part of the regiment. But if the soldier's family was rich, they could hire someone else to take their place. The only persons who would accept to take someone else's place were the people among the poor and the weak. The army then did not get the best-qualified soldiers.

The soldiers that served the army in the old system, chosen by *utskrivning* were paid a salary when they were at war, but in peace time the Crown could not afford to keep a standing army so the soldiers were sent home to take care of themselves as best as they could. Another problem with those involuntarily chosen soldiers was the large number of desertions. There was no standing army at this time except for the Lifeguard Regiments and for the Regiments that manned the fortresses around the nation. They were paid a salary.

The Old Allotment System initially, was a way to organize the armed forces even if the cavalry system was similar to the new system. (Hans Högman, Sollentuna, Sweden).

Johan Jonasson Enström
Grandfather to Harry Enstrom

Johan Jonsson was the third child and son of Jonas Anderson Qvist and Helena Eriksdotter. He was born on May 4, 1815 in Karlstorp Jonkoppings Parish. He died at the age of sixty- four years on September 14, 1879 in Hycklinge, Ostergotlands, Sweden of Tuberculosis.

At birth he was named Johan Jonasson (Jona's son) and in accordance with the naming practice in Sweden, however, once he moved out of his father's home and entered the military, he adopted the name of "Enström".

Johan married Anna Lisa Danielsdotter, the daughter of Daniel Christofferson and Maria Jonsdotter who was born on May 12, 1817 in Jareda Kalmar Parish and she died at eighty-eight years old on September 4, 1905 from old age.

Johan and Anna Lisa had six children:

I.   Maria Kristina Borb, born January 30, 1842 in Ekenäs Målilla and who died on January 12, 1906 at the age of sixty-four of Hemorrhagia cerebri (stroke);

II.   Jonas Peter, born December 17, 1843; he married Emilia Lewonii;

III.   Carl Johan born December 4, 1846;

IV.   Emma Gustafa born on October 12, 1849 and died at age sixty-four years on January 4, 1913 of cancer. She married Axel Gotfrid Karlsson on January 25, 1879;

V.   Frans Oscar born on April 7, 1855 in Tuna married Josephina Larsdotter on October 27,1883 in Gothenburg; and

VI.   Anna Lovisa, born June 2, 1860 in Svansdal

Parish and who died at the age of three on November 21, 1862 in Hycklinge Ostergotlands, of tonsilitis or diphtheria.

A large percentage of children died of the same illness that year.

The family moved to Tuna in 1855 but left directly thereafter for Hycklinge, Ostergotlands, where Johan became a private teacher. In 1857 they moved to Svanshalls, where he still worked as a private teacher then, in 1861 they returned to Hycklinge.

After the death of Johan, his wife Anna Lisa moved to live with her daughter Emma in Dalheim, then she moved to Oppeby, and was listed as a pauper in the 1890 Swedish Census. According to the Census in 1900 she was alone in Oppeby. The family had a history of poverty and disadvantage.

Johan Jonsson Enstrom with a height one hundred and sixty-seven centimetres, without ranking, was enlisted on May 28, 1835 at the age of twenty years as a *Husar* (Light Cavalryman) and lived in Målilla, Ekenäs, Hagatorp. His Croft File No. was S4-02-0059-1835. Regiment *Skaraborgs Regemente Company.*

Sweden had not been engaged in any wars since 1814 and hence Johan did not participate in any wars.

THE CENTRAL SOLDIERS REGISTER
Garnisonsmuseet
P.O Box 604
S-541 29 Skövde
SWEDEN
E-mail: bjorn.lippold@mil.se

Document number: SU-02-0059-1835

SOLDIER DOCUMENT

Regiment: Parish: **KARLSTORP**
Company: **SÖDRA VEDBO**   Atlas.
File: **Marholma**   Coordinate: X: Y:

Name: **ENGSTRÖM Johan**
Birth date: **4/5/1815**   Birth place: **Karlstorp**   County: F
Deceased: Place of death: County:
Age: Family name: Cause of death:
                                          Rank: **No ranking**
Height: **167**
Relatives.   Transport:
Enlisted: **8/28/1835**   Discharged: Years of service:

Father:
Occupation:
Mother:

Wife:
Birth date: Birth place: County:
Married date: Place: -   County: -
Deceased: Place of death: County:
Children: Birth date: Birth place:

Sources:

Notes:

The Soldiers Register is a secondary source. The user is responsible for verifying the
information against the original sources.
When quoting information from this register, attribute it to "Centrala soldatregistret".

THE CENTRAL SOLDIERS REGISTER
Garnisonsmuseet
P.O Box 604
S-541 29 Skövde

SWEDEN

Croft number: SU-02-0059

CROFT DOCUMENT

Regiment: Skaraborgs regemente
Company: SÖDRA VEDBO
Parish: KARLSTORP
Atlas:

File: Marholma
Croft name: Hagtorpet
Coordinate: X=   Y=

The cottage buildings   Share

Left: Demolished: Moved:

Other:

Barn: Basement: Yard: Well:

Photograph:

Notes: Smålands cavalry horse regiment have from beginning one regiment on thousand troops divided on eight company; the regiment where divide in whole Småland.
It where after year 1792 one light horse regiment and call from year 1801 Smålands light dragoon.
It divided year 1812 to two regiment, one whit horses and the other without.

Other soldiers who have lived in this croft

Filenumber	Name	Born	Deceased	Enlisted	Discharged
SU-02-0059-1833	HÄGG Lars	1796	0	1833	8/2/1834
SU-02-0059-1834	WANGLER Nils	1803	0	8/2/1834	5/28/1835
SU-02-0059-1835	ENGSTRÖM Johan	4/5/1815	0	5/28/1835	0

The Soldiers Register is a secondary source. The user is responsible for verifying the information against the original sources.
When quoting information from this register, attribute it to "Centrala soldatregistret".

Whilst it is known that Johan adopted the Croft name of *Enstrom,* Enström too is rather typical of the so-called "town names", used by people like craftsmen, merchants and civil servants (officials) who lived in towns and cities. The common practice for this class of people was to assume a name consisting of two parts which referred to "something in nature", very often starting off with a tree.

En-ström is most certainly Juniper + stream. Names like it abound in Swedish. Lind-gren, Linden branch; Ek-berg, oak mountain; Alm-qvist, elm twig, and many more variations on the theme.

Some regiments gave this sort of town name to its soldiers while others stuck to more typical martial names like Spjut, javelin; Lans, lance; or even Krig, war, but soldiers' names were not supposed to be retained by a soldier after he was discharged. It was very rare before the mid to late nineteenth century for a soldier's family to use his "soldier" name. The soldier name can be viewed more along the lines of a "badge of honour" but it could also have been likely that the origin of the name lies with some craftsman.

In both of these instances the names of *Qvist* and *Enstrom* were military names. In later years, the two little dots above the "o" in Enstrom were dropped.

Jonas Peter Enström
Father of Harry Enström

Jonas Peter Enstrom, also known as John, was the firstborn son of Johan Enstrom and Anna Lisa Danielsdotter. Born on December 17, 1843 in Mälilla in Kalmar Län, Småland, Sweden he moved to Stockholm in 1859. In 1869 he was registered as being employed as Sergeant in the Långholmen Prison and on October 7, 1871 he married Emilia Lewonii, daughter of book printer Christopher Lewonii and his wife Maria Elisabeth. The tax records after 1855, shows that Emilia who appears in 1871, is called a *travelling lady.*

According to Anders Isberg – Landsarkivet-lund-ra.se there are notes which consist of the names and birth dates of his family registered in the parish register of Landskrona Parish 1895 – 1899 (A11 a: 15 page 220) at Stottsstaten.

Landskrona Castle (*Citadellet Landskrona*) which was built in 1549 was located between Malmo and Helsingborg. During the nineteenth and twentieth centuries it was used as a refugee camp, a forced labour facility and even a women's prison. Jonas Peter Enstrom's occupation reads "*devaknings befälhavare*" which can be translated into "in charge of security/surveillance staff".

There is also a large prison in Varberg. It was in Varberg, that his daughter Signe Emilia was born, so Jonas was most likely working at that prison as well.

Harry's Siblings:

I.   Edith Ester Elizabeth Enstrom was shown as a single person in the Census of 1900;

II.   Erik Leonard Enstrom's occupation was *Garvaregesall* (Journeyman or Apprentice);

III.   Signe Emilia Enstrom married Carl Gustav Stabe;

IV.   Herta Alfhild Enstrom; unknown information.

Adventure Bound

"morgonstund bar guld: mund"
(Morning has gold in its mouth)

On a summer's morning in May 1889, a young boy sat in his bedroom in Stockholm, Sweden. He had got on his knees, and as usual, recited his morning prayer, the "Our Father".

Vår Fader, du som ä i himlen

Låt ditt namn bli helgat

Låt ditt rike komma

Låt din vilja ske på jorden så som I himlen

Ge oss I dag det bröd vi behöver

Och förlåtitt dem som står I skuld till oss

Och utsätt oss inte för pröving

Utan rädda oss från det onda

Ditt är riket

Din aä makten och äran

I evighet. Amen

He then sat back on his bed and as he glanced around the practical furnishings, a small, upholstered armchair, a table and a lamp, there was an explosion in his brain. He suddenly could feel the calling card of adventure; paths waiting for his feet; oceans waiting to be sailed. Whatever lie ahead could be a great challenge, tears, heartbreak, loneliness, and solitude. The thrill-seeking adventurous life which he yearned for required him to make decisions that would put his life at great risk.

As he laced his boots and took a step forward, buttoned up his jacket, adventure murmured to his soul, speaking of new things upon the horizon. Only a few minutes prior to this he had the patchwork quilt from his bed wrapped around his shoulders as a cape, as if the memories which his mother had given him had superpowers. He picked his way across the room to the doorway, and walked down the passage to the kitchen, looking forward to the usual *smörgås* (open faced sandwich) topped with cheese and jam. He slurped the coffee from the saucer through the lump of sugar between the teeth.

Harry embraced the elements, as he walked out of the square built, but picturesque cottage, in the densely populated village of Landskrona located on the shores of the Öresund, overlooking the river of clear water running along a bed of polished prehistoric egglike stones. Landskrona's excellent natural harbour with its extensive system of moats, constructed around the castle had military importance until the 1700s. The stone cottage that Harry and his family resided in was in the northern part of the *Citadellet*.

Harry had commenced school at seven years old and had completed eight years of primary education in exceptionally poor conditions. He was an average student, well behaved and self-motivated. His personality was well developed, and he showed an interest in everything; a jovial temperament possessing an indefatigable energy. Harry hated school. He wanted freedom to learn; he would school himself quicker than anyone else could teach him. He was now ready to accept responsibility for his own venturous and confident personality.

He came from a long line of soldiers who had served the crown in war and peace for well over two hundred years, however, he yearned to travel and from an incredibly young age, adventure was in his blood.

A likeable young lad with eyes of mischief and a heart of gold; enthusiastic, and fearless; he had the spark of a child and a smile that went all the way through to his core. He could have been beefier, but he was still well built for his tender age. For now, he was in search of independence and opportunity, albeit he was concerned for the fate of those who would be left behind. He loved his family. Harry, however, was on a mission.

Born on March 25, 1873, in Magdalena Parish, Stockholm City, Bror Emil Hjalmar Enstrom, (also known as Harry) was the son of Jonas Peter Enstrom, and Emilia Lewonii. Jonas and Emilia were married in Stockholm on October 7, 1871.

Harry's father had moved to Stockholm in 1859. In 1869 he took up the position of correctional Sergeant of Långholmen Prison one of the largest facilities in Sweden with more than five hundred cells. It was the location of the last execution in Sweden prior to the abolition of capital punishment in 1921. The prison operations dominated the island for two hundred and fifty years; the long and narrow island of Långholmen has traces of ancient habitations dating back to the tenth century and, in the heart of Stockholm, is now a green island. The prison closed in 1975 and in 1989 opened as a hotel and youth hostel.

Jonas and Emilia settled in Stockholm where their first three children were born in the Maria Magdalena Parish, viz;

I.   Edith Ester Elizabeth – born in 1872;

II.   Bror Emil Hjalmar – born in 1873; and

III.   Erik Leonard – born in 1875.

Later the family moved to Varberg County, Province of Halland where a fourth child;

IV.   Signe Emilia was born in 1879;

V.   A fifth child, Hertha Alfhild was born in 1884

        in Landskrona City, County of Malmohus,

        Province of Skåne.

Jonas Peter (father), Emilia (mother), Edith Ester, Bror Emil Hjalmar, Signe Emilia, Erik Leonard and Hertha Alfhild.

This was the family of Harry.

Harry the Seaman

"A sailor is not defined as much by how many seas he has sailed,
Than by how many storms he has overcome".
Matshona Dhliwayo
Zimbabwean Philosopher, Entrepreneur and Writer

Harry often sat with his Grandfather, Johan Jonsson Enstrom and listened to the tales of war and travels. He relished and became encouraged by all the stories of adventure that his Grandfather told him.

He also knew that life on the whaleships was going to be tough. A skipper could thrash a cabin boy for even the smallest mistake so the only solution open to these young boys, sometimes as young as fourteen years old, was to jump ship; crew who disobeyed orders could be thrashed with the cat-o-nine-tails. This did not deter him.

It was still early one morning in June 1889 when, with cap on his head, he walked out of the cottage emerging onto the densely populated street, dodging heavy traffic, horse carts and open trams as he headed for the shipping office. On the way all sorts of things were going through this youngster's head. He recalled how the family frequented the fishing settlement of Sønder Sæby; fishing being a favourite pastime. He wondered whether he would ever experience this happy time with his family again.

He finally found his way to the shipping office, entered, and was greeted by the shipping clerk.

"God morgon herrn", (good morning sir).

After some discussion Harry enrolled as a deck boy at the Shipping Office in Landskrona. He was elated. He jumped for joy and double somersaulted as he arrived home that afternoon. He could not wait to tell his parents that he had a job.

As a seagull hopped over the quay as if too lazy to spread its grey-white wings, Harry, fair hair, gleaming blue eyes, well groomed, with a skip in his step, turned for the jetty. The time had come. What was the fresh-faced young boy doing on the docks? A large suitcase with his belongings standing on the dock next to him. Before he left home that morning his father had entered the room and handed him a thick warm jacket, woolen balaclava, and gloves.

"Ta den här med dig, du kommer att behöva den" (Take these with you, you will need them).

His father, mother, and siblings, with feelings of concern, were at his side. His father showing strength, his Mother with a tear in her eye.

At the sight of the boat mooring, Harry's heart missed a beat. A young boy of fourteen years of age, standing on the shore looking out over the surface of the sea of unfathomable depths, could only try to visualize where the monsters of the sea swam; wonder and marvel at the beauty, power, and mystery. He felt the excitement, butterflies in his stomach as the signal was given; departure was at hand.

He had enrolled as a deck boy at the Shipping Office in Landskrona, on Wednesday, June 12, 1889, on the *Brig Galathea* and sailed to Nyham, Höganäs. His salary was 12 crowns per month. As the boat left the Landskrona harbor, he had a lot going on in his mind, after all he was still only a child.

He travelled the deep and dangerous, rollicking high seas on the *Brig Galatheo*, a two square-masted sailing vessel, which was not only used as a small war ship but also as a standard cargo ship due to its maneuverability, but which required a large crew to handle.

Harry soon learnt that life on the whaleship was isolated; albeit that a typical crew of a sailing ship consisted of sixteen to seventeen men; the Captain, First Mate, Second Mate, Boatswain, Ship's Carpenter, Cook, nine to ten able and ordinary seamen, and of course the "boy". (norwayheritage.com)

In the calm waters that had prevailed so far, the boat had maintained a slow but steady progress. He would experience the calm seas, likened to a peaceful lake, where the broad back of the granite like whales breached in the sunlight in near view, drawing a long breath. This was when the air vibrated with the rhythmic pounding of waves as they plunged down into their home. He would feel the white salt spray that came crashing over the gunwale and whipped his ruddy cheeks. A young deckhand, who had been reading about the monsters since he was extremely young, now somewhere deep in the ocean, were the monsters and he would have his own stories to take home.

It was not long before the wind was rising, and the ocean swells were building. The crew did not need anyone to tell them that a storm was coming, that was obvious. He soon found that as the dark clouds of the brewing storm obscured the moon, the boat heaved and tossed on the rising swell; the boat rolling from side to side as the temperature suddenly dropped. In this unfamiliar environment he was scared. His thoughts suddenly were of home, the warm cozy bed, and the family gatherings around the fire; for now, he would experience being seasick for the first time. The sickness came in waves, he rushed for fresh air, but there was no relief from the retchings, the acrid return of the greasy meat which he had had for dinner; for now, he was crippled by sea sickness. As he tried to lean over the side a fellow mariner offered him a jug of rum. He had never had alcohol before and tried to refuse.

"Come on lad, get some of this into ya".

Harry procrastinated, but in desperation took a swig from the earthern-ware flagon. Soon he was cured.

The smile on his face said it all, "Remarkable, I can now walk on water".

He gradually progressed and on May 6, 1893 was enrolled as a seaman *(sjoman)* at a salary of forty crowns per month on the ship *Beda*, operated by Charles Brower, which had previously sailed from Landskrona to Canada and arrived in the Arctic in the year 1885. Again, he would experience storms that came roaring in out of the Antarctic, in a fury of wind and ice whipping the waters of the sea into a maelstrom. It was where the air was so cold, minus twenty, but the surging winds made it feel more like fifty. He snuggled as much as he could into his warm jacket. How he appreciated this gift from his father.

This was where Charles Brower opened his own whaling operation, the Cape Smythe Whaling and Trading Company at Barrow, Alaska. Interestingly, Swedish whaling also existed, though not nearly at the same scale as in Norway, Iceland, or Great Britain. In the eighteenth century there were several Swedish whaling companies often operating from Gothenburg, but these had barely started at the time frame when Harry was a seaman.

Harry again enrolled on May 29, 1891 as a deck boy at the Schooner *Oskar* from Råå, Helsingborg. His salary was thirty crowns per month. The Schooner *Oskar* sailed from Landskrona to Lubeck in Germany. Subsequently he re-enrolled as a seaman on the *Brig Galatheo* which sailed from Landskrona to Port Natal in South Africa by Sundsvall in the northern part of Sweden.

For years Harry worked on the whaling vessels in the Arctic and an area which expanded well into the Indian and Pacific Oceans. Once on board, wearing overalls, balaclava, and canvas shoes, he joined the plight of the helpless sailors. His weathered face always on the lookout. Decades in the open air, in all weathers, his skin had become tanned and thicker than most men of his age. It was the calloused hands, the eyes, cloudy and grey, rather than blue, that told the stories of the raging storms, the stress, and the trauma.

He found that daily life on the whaleship sometimes ranged from repulsive to horrendous. The food was terrible as the crew were served with anything from oleaginous pork to dried biscuits. The only time that the food was good was on Christmas Day when they ate at the Captain's table. The only fresh food and fruit that was served was when ships called into the ports. The crew also were housed in the fo'c'e'sle, in sailor's parlance, or the forecastle.

He would endure quarters which were small, black with grungy filth and extremely hot; they were filled with a compound of foul air, stale smoke and vermin. Many years later Harry would still have nightmares about rats in his pillow. Seamen could be away for years as they roamed the oceans of the world.

There were the times too when Harry marveled as the majestic whales came up for air; but felt distressed as they breached the surface, and he heard the explosive crack sound; then a thud, as the harpoon slammed into the head penetrating half a meter deep. The defenseless whale trying to pull away, terrified and in agony, as the grenade inside the harpoon exploded blasting shrapnel into the body. This senseless killing would be repeated, over and over, again.

To capture whales, provided the most dangerous and hardest life ever possible. Could this honestly be what these young men were looking for when they were looking for *adventure?*

The whaling era had inflicted an enormous assault on the barnacle encrusted forty-ton warm blooded mammals. The clash of whale and boat, wrestling and grappling with this thing brought terror that dwelt in the bowels, hunting down this beast required everything that they had to give. The seamen who worked on these vessels, did so under the most dangerous conditions not only from the high seas and weather but also, once the harpoons were exploded, the harpooned whale could overturn the boat or cause great damage during its final moments in the death flurry; under the worst of conditions the industry survived. At the time, whale blubber was a valuable and sought-after commodity.

The hardship and trauma were daily occurrences on these vessels, and it was when Harry's best friend became the victim of a "man overboard" who could not be retrieved, and a second friend who broke his leg, as the ship broadsided on a wave, that he could no longer cope with the dangerous life which was on offer. He often sat and thought about the consequences, it only took one reckless moment for a seaman to end up in a watery grave. The stress felt as the vessel moved through the depths of the ocean was when sailors became aware of the currents and schools of the living as, knuckles white, they held tight to the iron railings.

The roving whalers opened the world, however, on a beautiful spring evening in September 1899, the Brig *Galatheo*, under the command of the captain, sailed up the eastern seaboard of southern Africa, and moored overnight in the lee of the Bluff headland. Early the next morning, the boat slipped through the entrance to the harbour and offloaded its cargo at the slipway. These ill-fated whale carcasses were dragged up the slipway and on to the low bed rail cars of the steam tank locomotives, and transported to the old whaling station and factory on the Bluff.

Harry had, over the previous days, made up his mind that when the *Galatheo* docked in the natural harbour of Durban he would pack his bags and abandon ship.

As Harry made his way to the Harbour Hideaway in Durban, an historical landmark built in 1899, he looked forward to meeting up with seamen from the world over. It was where he met up with acquaintances with whom he had crossed paths many times before. Ships were also sailing into Durban harbour, one of the major ports in Africa, with British troops who were part of the "Imperial" Contingents and as Harry had longed to break free from his confines, he saw the advent of the Anglo Boer War as the ideal opportunity.

During his frequent visits to the Harbour Hideaway over the forthcoming days he also met up with a past acquaintance, Carl Johnson, whom he had met on many occasions.

Ironically, the story of Carl Johnson was extraordinarily, akin to that of Harry. Carl too came from a long line of soldiers who had served the crown in war and peace for many years. Carl left school at the age of eleven, however, he was brought back and given a thrashing. When he turned twelve, he made his final bid for freedom. He made his way to the sea, believed to be at Gothenburg and got a berth in a windjammer as a cabin boy in 1879. He jumped ship in Cape Town and managed to flee out to the Cape Flats where he was given shelter by a Boer farmer. He somehow then took another ship as it was recalled that he again jumped ship in Malmö,

Sweden. Carl did manage to progress through the grades and learnt a lot of skills in navigation.

Carl realised early that he would never make a fortune just as a plain seafaring skipper and looked for other opportunities which included ventures in the States without success. He ended up back in South Africa and his dream of financial success included the tourist potentialities in the colourful Zulu ricksha boys in Durban, and it was not long before he imported rickshas from Japan.

Unlike Harry, who had enlisted in the Anglo Boer War, Carl, who was much older, was given food for thought when he saw the Norwegian whaling station in Durban, and he became interested in the fishing and whaling industry, eventually taking delivery of several trawlers and fisheries survey ships. Carl eventually became one of the magnates of the fishing giants Irvin and Johnson. (Sound of Jura – source document Margaret Cox (Melbourne) Recorded by Carl Johnson's daughter Esther Oceana Greenwood (nee Johnson). Permission given by Glenn Mcintosh to use the article).

At the Harbour Hideaway in Durban, Harry would ultimately listen to all the yarns, tell tall tales himself and this was where he heard that recruits were required to enlist in the Anglo Boer War. This would be the next stage in the adventurous life which he craved. Harry soon found his way to the Victoria Barracks and signed as a volunteer.

In 1899 the Swedish Census showed that the family, including Harry, were living in Landskrona where Harry's father, John, was working as a Security Officer at the Landskrona Castle, *citadellet.* In 1901, two years after having gone "absent without leave" Harry was removed from the enrolment lists.

It must be questioned, however, that once he left Sweden as a young man, whether he ever did have the chance of seeing his family again?   The home, featuring classic Nordic décor, with beige and grey walls, roof to floor curtains, that he left on that rather warmish June morning as an ordinary young fourteen-year-old boy, who would travel on his own journey through a metamorphosis, from being an ordinary boy to a hero. One can only wonder.

The Anglo Boer War

When the war of the giants is over
The wars of the pygmies will begin.
Winston Churchill

Harry Enstrom

Money, or the lack of it, played a large part in the decision to try life in the colonies. Emigration, one of the most dramatic life changes anyone undertook, was becoming a popular route to a better way of life for young men of all classes and backgrounds. When war broke out, Bror Emil Hjalmar Enstrom, also known as Harry, was recorded as a Naturalised British Citizen on enlistment with the British Army in October 1899 in Durban. He signed up for service in the Second Anglo Boer War and was assigned to the Bethune's Mounted Infantry, a Volunteer Unit raised in Durban, Natal, South Africa in October 1899 under Major E.C. Bethune of the Queen's 16th Lancers. Major E.C. Bethune, an officer was to do well during the entirety of the war, like several others who undertook the raising and command of irregular corps before the value of these was fully appreciated.

It has been well documented that the Anglo Boer War which broke out in late 1899 all initially started from the Gold rush in the Transvaal. Large numbers of "outlanders" (foreigners) flocked to the Transvaal and established an English community amid a rural Boer society. Paul Kruger saw this as a threat to the separate national identity of his people; "God's People" as he called them. The mining magnates of Johannesburg criticized Kruger's economic and railway policy, which was aimed at promoting the independence of the Transvaal, but which resulted at the same time in raising the cost of the production of gold.

On the other hand, Cecil Rhodes, The Cape Premier, who had large gold interests and much political influence, hoped to achieve a united British South Africa. When he failed to persuade Kruger to join a South African union, he decided to bring matters to a head. Ever since 1890 he also had had to cope with growing opposition from some of his own people. In May 1899, a conference took place in Bloemfontein, between Kruger and Milner who had been sent to South Africa as governor of the Cape Colony. Although no agreement was reached, Kruger decided on a seven-year residential qualification. Milner refused the offer.

In summarising, faced with pressure from the British High Commissioner, Alfred Milner, needed to liberate the *uitlanders* who flocked to the South African Republic after the discovery of gold in 1886, however, the Boer Republic's President, Paul Kruger, decided to fight.

War broke out and although the Boer had initial successes, British invading armies occupied the two Boer capitals. Kruger was forced to retreat with the last Boer army along the Delagoa Bay railway. Being too old to keep up the struggle, he was delegated to Europe where he lived in Holland to the end of the war in 1902. He died in Switzerland in July 1904 and his body found a provisional resting place at the Hague. He was finally buried at Pretoria on December 16, 1904.

As Harry was attached to the Bethune's Mounted Infantry, it was interesting to note that the history of The Queen's 16th Lancers, started as early as 1759 being involved in several wars including the war against France in 1793, Waterloo in 1815 and of course World Wars 1 and II.

Once Harry received his kit he was immediately seconded to duties. Wearing the Foreign Service helmet, complete with hat badge, khaki tunic, shoulder title "B.M.I" (Natal), rifle, cloth made bandolier with pockets for ammunition, canteen holding about one and a half litres of water and mess tin, Harry was equipped for duty. (The Anglo Boer War and related history group). Interestingly, the South African Mounted Irregular Forces were viewed inconsistently by many in the Regular Army. Among other regiment's nicknames, Bethune's Mounted Infantry were irreverently nicknamed "Bethune's Buccaneers". (A History of the British Cavalry. Vol.4 1899 – 1913 by the Marquess of Anglesey (1986) p.71).

Harry, being an early colonial recruit meant that he would have been one of the first who attested with Bethune's Mounted Infantry for service from the inception in Durban, as was Trumpeter Wilson, No. 114, on October 19, 1899. They had been on the move ever since they had mobilised in Durban on that date.

He would soon find that the physical conditions of a country were so far removed from his hometown in Sweden. He relished the Durban warm subtropical climate and beautiful beaches, but he also had to contend with the dry and arid veld.

In following the trail which Harry was on, the regiment was ultimately present at General Hildyard's action at Willow Grange on the night of November 22, 1899 and did good service. At Colenso on December 15, 1899 the five hundred strong regiment, of which thirty-nine were Australian, was present but was detailed as portion of the baggage guard.

It was during the time spent in the camp that Harry's mind wandered; what was happening at home in Sweden as it was not long before Christmas. His mother would prepare the most lavish meal of the year to be had on Christmas Eve. This was always the promise of the year's largest feast to chase away the gloom. He started salivating as he thought of the pickled herrings and boiled potatoes followed by baked ham, red cabbage cooked with apples and rye bread. The almond tarts filled with whipped cream as dessert. He also smiled as he thought of his younger years when he and his siblings left milk and cookies out for Santa and put out a dish of rice pudding to appease the house gnome.

He thought too of the night when friends and family gathered around the hearth. The dark evenings lit by the light of Advent candles in the window. The warmth of hot mulled wine and the yeasty smell of fresh baked saffron bread, these brought on nostalgia which was hard to shake.

Harry would, however, for now enjoy the chocolates, packed in a commemorative tin, which Queen Victoria had gifted to the British troops serving in the Boer War. There was nothing like a tin of melting chocolates under the African sun as he took pleasure in savouring these.

The year 1899 had ended well for the British but what was to follow in the New Year? What was he doing here? The flies were everywhere, he was finding it hard to cope with the dust which had thickly built up in everything, on this scorching December day in Natal, thousands of miles from his home. Water was short as was food, which consisted mainly of bread and bully beef. Horses were already being slaughtered and made into sausages, soup and processed in bottles of Chervil to feed the troops. Bethune's Mounted Infantry had been dubbed as "Bethune's Buccaneers", as there were those who had stolen stores to survive.

On January 24, 1900 awful blood shed was going on upon the summit of Spion Kop, Colonel Bethune with two of his squadrons were to assist. However, the Bethune's Mounted Infantry were kept in reserve by General Talbot Coke as he was of the opinion, that the lining of the trenches was rather that of the infantry, the 3rd King's Royal Rifles and the Scottish Rifles, which were already present. It was at Spion Kop, and Potgietersdrift, that Mahatma Gandhi's Natal Indian Volunteer Ambulance Corps provided service transporting the wounded to field hospitals. (The Anglo Boer War and related history Group)

February the fifth, saw the capture of the Vaal Krantz operations. During this time, the Corps continued to do patrol work chiefly on General Buller's right and rear.

On February 11, 1900 Colonel Bethune was ordered to take his men to Greytown with instructions to watch the Boers near the Zululand border, plus with the view of ultimately co-operating from Greytown in any movements towards Dundee. The regiment thus missed the fierce fighting which took place near Colenso between the 13th and 27th February 1900. On February 28, 1900, after one hundred and twenty days, the siege of Ladysmith was lifted, and the besieged residents and military units were saved. (Anglo Boer War and related history group)

Before Laing's Nek was turned, Bethune's Mounted Infantry were to suffer a grievous mishap. Col. Bethune with about five hundred men from Dundee had been detached on May 19, 1899 on the instructions of General Buller to march to Nqutu and to re-join at Newcastle. When General Buller attempted to turn the right of the Boer positions between himself and Ladysmith, Bethune's Mounted Infantry was split up. One squadron being left under General Barton at Frere and Chieveley, where they were employed on reconnaissance duties and had several casualties. The remainder of the corps accompanied their commander to Potgieter's Drift where they were attached to General Lyttleton's Brigade, also being involved in skirmishes on various occasions.

Bethune's Mounted Infantry consisting of three hundred and fifty-six British Soldiers, two artillery guns, under the command of Colonel Edward Cecil Bethune, were advancing to Vryheid from Nqutu. Other officers in the group were Captain Goff, Captain Ford, Lieutenant McLachlan, and Lieutenant Lantham. The British were informed that the Boer forces had already left Vryheid so they were advancing to Vryheid to clean up whatever may have been left of the Boer forces and capture any needed supplies.

Against the orders of Colonel Bethune, and persistent to carry out his orders to raid Vryheid, Colonel Goff moved too far ahead of the rest of the advancing column and thereby isolated his squadron.

It was early on a cold Sunday morning May 20, 1900 at Scheeper's Nek near Vryheid where approximately ninety Boers gathered in silence. The only voice that could be heard was that of the Field Chaplin, Dominee Edwin Cheere Anderson. The Boer Commander had chosen the position well; a rocky outcrop about fifty meters from a natural spring and slightly higher than the transport route from Dundee to Vryheid which passed them close by. Scouts were out and about a few hundred meters away being on the lookout for enemy approach. About midway through conducting his service the preacher was rudely disrupted by the abrupt arrival of a scout in among the group of church goers, hat in his hand, rifle in the other.

"More, Dominee Kommandant, die Engelse is hier!" (Morning Pastor Commandant, the English are here!).

The Boer General, Chris Botha, had issued an instruction to Commandant Blignaut of the Swaziland Police under the command of the Commandant Jacobus Danieel "Koot" Opperman, together with eighty Burghers, to occupy Scheeper's Nek and to await the British advance to Vryheid. (S.A. Military History Society)

Unfortunately, one of the English officers of the advance squadron of Bethune's Mounted Infantry rode up to the Boer guards without noticing them, giving them the opportunity to disperse before the British could attack.

The Boers were lying in wait in two farmhouses on the west side of the Nek area and from some stony kopjes on the eastern side. The morning winter sun also in their favor, shining directly into the faces of whoever would be a traveler to Vryheid at that point. Folklore has it that Dominee Anderssen had right there exchanged his Bible for a rifle and was in among his fellow Burghers waiting for the British to arrive.

It was an intense battle that lasted less than an hour. All were caught by surprise. The first thing that the ill-fated English probably became aware of, were the orange flashes of Mauser fire and the whizzing and whining of ricocheting bullets. Captain Goff, who was in command of the leading squadron which was considerably in advance of the rest of the force, found himself in an exposed position on a slope where ant heaps formed the only cover. The Boers deployed to ridges on the east and north and their fir created havoc amongst the British horses. The dismounted infantry replied as best they could and made good use of the Maxim gun. The first to be gunned down were the British officers who were on horseback at the very front of the column.

Harry, who was in the squadron, was involved in the skirmish which took place at Scheeper's Nek, ten kilometres south west of Vryheid in Natal, and sadly on Sunday, May 20, 1900 he received gunshot wounds to the chest, shoulder and buttock, when a squadron of Col E.C. Bethune, under Capt. Goff, 3rd Dragoon Guards, ran into a well-placed Boer ambush under Com. Blignaut.

Suddenly, Harry still on horseback, felt that he had been kicked extremely hard with a heavy boot. As he fell to the ground, fearless Harry suddenly felt the pain; shock that he had been hit by enfilading fire. At the time he had heard the shockingly loud blasts, explosions, hundreds of loud bangs, and the repetitive dug-dug-dug hammering of the Maxim at 460 rounds per minute and saw the numerous muzzle flashes. There was complete mayhem and confusion as he lay there injured in the dust listening to the screams and yells of his fellow troopers. His horse lay a few metres away; dead. In his stupor, as he looked around all that he could see were khaki helmets crushed, bloodstained, and riddled with holes. Men crying and groaning everywhere. Only a few hours before, in the dew of the morning, the men had confidently marched out to battle.

Once the skirmish had terminated, the injured were taken by stretcher bearers to horse drawn wagons to be transported to field aid posts. Once under cover, the English medical orderlies/stretcher bearers moved in and treated the wounded of both sides using a field dressing, which each soldier was issued with and which had been sewn into a khaki cotton pouch and labelled FIRST AID DRESSING; the first war in which it happened. (Military History Journal. Vol. 6 No. 3 – June 1984.) The woollen pad infused with 3% cyanide of mercury and zinc, gauze bandages, an ampoule of iodine and two safety pins were utilized. Ligatures to slow the bleeding, pressure bandages and splints to immobilize limbs too were used.

Harry was aware of the Chaplain who had been travelling with the squadron offering water; in his inertness he heard him praying with the dying.

"Oh God am I going to die?"

After being treated at a mobile field hospital (space designed for ground sheets only for 100 patients), Harry was later transferred to a military hospital as he had sustained traumatic damage to flesh, nerves, bones, and organs. Foreign matter, dirt, cloth, and leather which had been forced into the wound cavities had caused infection. Attending to Harry in the hospital was a young nurse, Hilda, Kangela van Breda. This hazel eyed beauty, brown shoulder length hair tucked up into a white cap, red cape over her shoulders, white uniform with a red cross on the sleeve, and apron, would a few years later become his wife.

The British loss at Scheeper's Nek, was twenty-seven killed, twenty-five wounded, eleven taken prisoner and twenty-nine horses killed. The Boers captured a machine gun and twenty-six horses, while losing one burgher killed, one wounded and one captured by the British. The British withdrew with haste in the direction of Nqutu.

In his telegram of May 21, 1900 General Buller said that he had detached Col. Bethune with about five hundred men from Dundee on the 9th to march to Nqutu, and to re-join at Newcastle. On the 20th one squadron was ambushed about six miles south of Vryheid, very few escaping. Captain Goff, 3rd Dragoon Guards, Lieutenants Lanham and McLachlan, and about 26 non-commissioned officers and men, were killed.

The War Reporter, Weekly Edition, dated 26 May 1900 read:

"Volksrust, 25 May. Here on the Natal front, the Republican forces held their positions easily this week. In addition, the Burghers scored a decisive victory over a British patrol on 20 May at Scheepersnek, about 10 kilometres southwest of Vryheid." (S.A. Military History Society).

Bethune's mounted Infantry was during the remainder of 1900 mainly employed on patrol work in the south of the Transvaal and in the Utrecht district, with the view of protecting British posts and the railway line, frequently becoming involved in dangerous skirmishes.

It is understood that Vryheid was not damaged in the war, however, General Botha's farmhouse was blown up and was never replaced.

From all accounts Harry was one of eleven who were taken prisoner as in the Times Newspaper (U.K.) of July 21, 1900 Harry Enstrom was listed together with the names of other prisoners, who on July 24, 1900 were handed back to the British by the Boers under a *Flag of Truce.*

On October 7, 1900 medical records showed:

"I, Harry Enstrom, Trooper in the B.M.I. hereby affirm on oath that my domicile is in Durban, Natal". This was signed at Howick in Natal.

The Medical Report stated that he had considerable loss of power in his right leg; he complained of frequent dull pain in the lower part of abdomen and a difficulty in moving. Treatment consisted of rest and massage over the wound in the right hip. He was in the General Hospital at Howick and the proceedings revealed that he was twenty-seven years old, had eleven months service as No. 289 Trooper, Enstrom H., Bethune's Mounted Infantry. Their findings: "He is suffering from the effects of gunshot wounds of the chest, left shoulder and right hip and recommend his discharge as unfit for the Imperial Irregular Forces. The disability will prevent his earning a livelihood the extent of one third disability".

On December 22, 1900 Harry was transferred from Howick General Hospital to the *S.S.Formosa* Hospital at Sea, his destination, England. On board were six laying down patients, three hundred and thirty-two convalescent and twenty-one wounded convalescent patients plus officers on their way home. Civil surgeons A.F. Llot, H.L. Porteus, Nursing Sisters: A. Murton, A.F. Bob, M.M. Knox, and F Baker accompanied the wounded and sick and were on duty for the duration of the voyage. (angloboerwar.com/shipping records). He arrived at Woolwich on January 17, 1901. His religion was shown as

Church of England. It was recorded that bullets were lodged in the body but could not be found.

On June 17, 1901 he was sent to Bartholomew's Hospital for further treatment. On June 21, 1901 a detailed Medical History of an invalid written at Woolwich Hospital stated that:

"His age was recorded as twenty-eight and his former Occupation was that of Clerk. His disability was gunshot wounds chest, shoulder and buttock which disability originated on May 20, 1900 at Scheeper's Nek when, in action he received gunshot wounds. One entered right chest below the nipple and emerged behind one inch and a half to the left of the spine, another entered behind the left shoulder and there is no exit wound, though x-rays do not reveal the presence of a bullet. He was also wounded in the right buttock and over the spine above the folds of the buttock. Whether those are two entrance wounds, or one is an exit wound is impossible to determine. After exercise he suffers from severe abdominal pains with shooting pains down the legs and he finds great difficulty in straightening his back after he has been sitting for some time".

"The disease is the result of service, attributed to exposure on duty when in action and has not been aggravated by intemperance or misconduct. The disability is permanent. It will prevent his earning a full livelihood to extent of half. He was X-Rayed with negative results and no operative treatment was considered advisable. He was proposed for discharge on account of permanent unfitness for service". He was discharged from service on July 29, 1901 at Shorncliffe.

He was twenty-eight years of age, five feet, seven inches in height, chest measurement thirty- eight inches. His complexion was fair with blue eyes and light brown hair. Whilst still in England his intended place of residence: 17 Percy Street, Tottenham Ct Road, London WC.

On March 29, 1903 it was recorded that his wounds were completely healed but that he complained of pains in different parts of body, and it is possible that there is a bullet lodged as there is no exit aperture from his third wound in his buttock. The patient was lame from stiffness in left hip, not permanent, will improve, probable minimum duration six months.

On February 14, 1903, a Medical Report carried out in Durban stated that:

"Employment cited as De Waal and Co., Point, Durban: Foreman at 10/- a day".

Report (undated) states that his wounds remain healed, he suffers, as patient states from pains (vague) in chest which come on suddenly on any exertion, except slow walking. His heart seems to stop beating for a moment or two on such occasions. He has no lameness, the only physical sign detected is the slight irregularity in the heart's action. He smokes but not to excess. The irregular heart's action possibly permanent but will improve to a great extent. Wounds completely healed, not equal to the loss of a limb.

If patient can get a situation like his former one of overseer of natives, his capacity for earning a livelihood is hardly impaired at all but at manual labour, his capacity would be impaired to the extent of quarter fully".

The Boer War, according to Rudyard Kipling, taught the British "no end of a lesson". Thomas Packenham, author of the "Boer War" called it the longest, costliest, bloodiest and most humiliating war for Britain between 1815 – 1914.

Today none of us would have any idea of the hardships that these soldiers suffered. The lack of food and exercise, contaminated water and life underground soon bred fever, its victims outnumbered those of the Long Tom nearly ten to one. (Richard Harding Davis With Both Armies.)

Of course, the Military "commandeered" all available food. They seized hens, cows, and all kinds of eatables for which they paid a fair price, and which were reserved for all. Everyone, without distinction, was on fixed rations. In time two thousand horses were killed and served instead of beef. Canary seed was beaten up into meal and made into cakes. More pitifully when garrisons could no longer feed the horses, they were killed and eaten. In a war with human suffering there were their fellow sufferers, the horses.

Finally, the Peace Treaty was signed at Vereeniging on May 31, 1902. Harry was discharged after the war to remain in South Africa.

Whether Harry was admitted to the General Hospital in Howick immediately upon release is unknown, however, the proceedings of a Medical Board on October 7, 1900 revealed that he was "twenty-seven years old, had eleven months service as No. 289 Trooper H Enstrom, Bethune's Mounted Infantry". The Medical Board recommended his discharge as being unfit for the Imperial Irregular Forces because of the gunshot wounds which he had suffered.

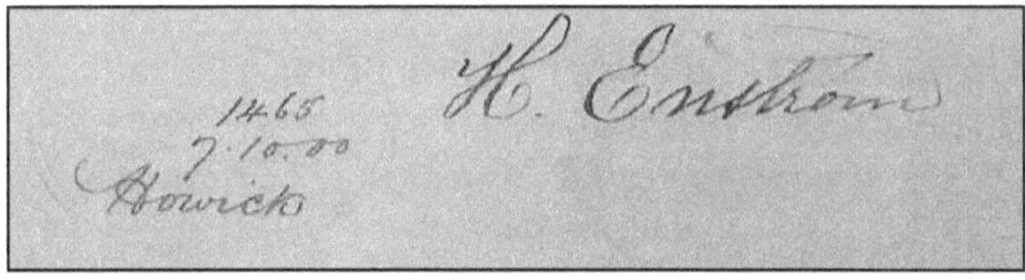

Detailed medical reports show that he was discharged from Service on July 29, 1901 at Shorncliffe, however, actual discharge would not be affected until 1906. His wishes were that he be returned to South Africa. This request was granted.

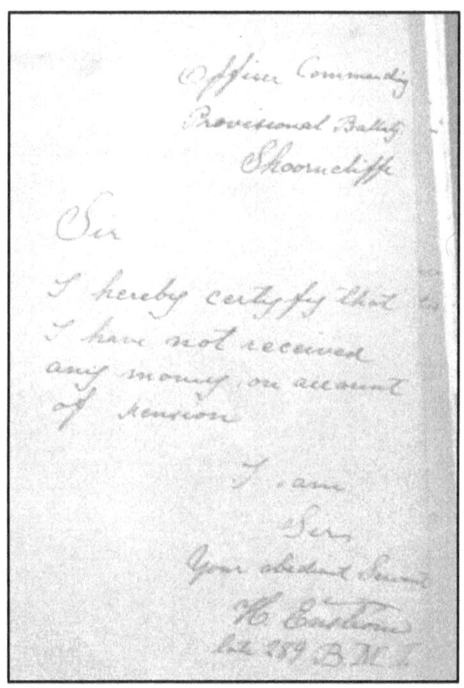

Undated letter signed by Harry Enstrom

One Hundredth Centenary – Battle of Scheepers' Nek

In my dreams I hear again the crash of guns, the rattle of
musketry,
The strange, mournful mutter of the battlefield.
Douglas MacArthur

In a letter received from Debbie Lynn Boock:

Just wanted to say thank you for all the hard work you put
into the Enstrom book - it has us fascinated!! We were very
interested to read about Sara Suzanna Ziervogel who lived and
died in Vryheid - the town where we live. My husband Carl
(Tempest and Adolf's son) who was a trooper in the Natal
Mounted Rifles, played the bugle at the one hundredth year
commemoration of the Battle of Scheeper's Nek (which is
about 10 kms from Vryheid) not knowing that his great
grandfather was wounded in the battle...Thanks again for all
the research! We appreciate it Debbie Boock.

Carl Boock and his Family at the Centenary Monument

In the Afrikaans language magazine "KEUR" of 26
February 1999, an article was written by the then Chief

Researcher of the War Museum in Bloemfontein, Elria Wessels, under the heading "Die geveg by Scheepersnek 20 Mei 1900". She wrote that while Bethune's Mounted Infantry were en route to Newcastle, Bethune received word from his African Scouts that the Vryheid district was basically left abandoned, and he then made the decision to go via Vryheid to seize the "large stores of all sorts". Wessels also writes that the British had been warned that the Boers were lying in wait but decided to ignore the warning.

A monument was erected about one kilometer from the actual battle site where the remains of the killed British officers, NCO's and soldiers were buried in a mass grave.

In May 2001, a one-hundred-year commemoration of the Battle of Scheeper's Nek was held on an adjacent farm *Strathcona*, attended by about five hundred people including some descendants of the soldiers who fell at Scheeper's Nek. (S.A. Military History Society.)

Carl Boock, great grandson of Harry who had played the bugle, was unaware that his great grandfather was wounded in the battle and had been taken Prisoner of War. **Carl wrote:**

> *"We went to the cemetery to see if we could find Sara Susanna Ziervogel's grave – unfortunately the old graves are all in between the new ones. Found the graves of Cheers Emmett (the Irish Boer General) and Lukas Meyer (the first President of the new Republic of Vryheid) as well as the graves of more members of the Bethune's Mounted Infantry killed at Blood River, and other skirmishes around Vryheid.*

Here is some information on the Vryheid Commandos. P.V. Scholtz was the great uncle of my late friend Peter Scholtz who has passed away. I met him in Durban in 1980 after completing two years military service in 1 SSB. His late father had been in the original 1 SSB under Poppa Britz. Great Grandpa Enstrom was probably fighting against Peter's family. He was the one who got me to Vryheid. My friend, like his great uncle, was a military person. All the MOTHS and Commandos were at his funeral. A lone piper played Sarie Marais, his last request. Peter's humor, as in the original Afrikaans words, Jannie Boer runs off to Upington to escape the Khakis English and can't return as a traitor as Sarie will reward him with a coffin. Peter was called the Viking as he was 6.6 had red hair and beard and the temperament of the Norse but was a master artisan. Regards the question are we related to the Vikings? Maybe looking at the artisan skills, the love of the sea, boats, and fishing there is definitely Norse blood. My dad's family came from Denmark; since I was a child, I imagined myself as a Viking. I remember playing vikings with my cousin."

One hundredth Centenary Monument at Scheeper's Nek

Scheeper's Nek 1995: The old wagon road in a view looking to the west. This is the precise spot where "E" Squadron was ambushed and shot down by Boer rifle fire from the rocky outcrop out of sight to the left of the picture. This area has now been planted with timber and there are no visible traces of the old road.

List of Casualties

The remains of the killed British Officers, NCOs and soldiers were buried in a mass grave with a separate small monument for Sergeant Major Schmitt Hadley.

Scheeper's Nek 1995: The rocky outcrop which overlooks the old road.

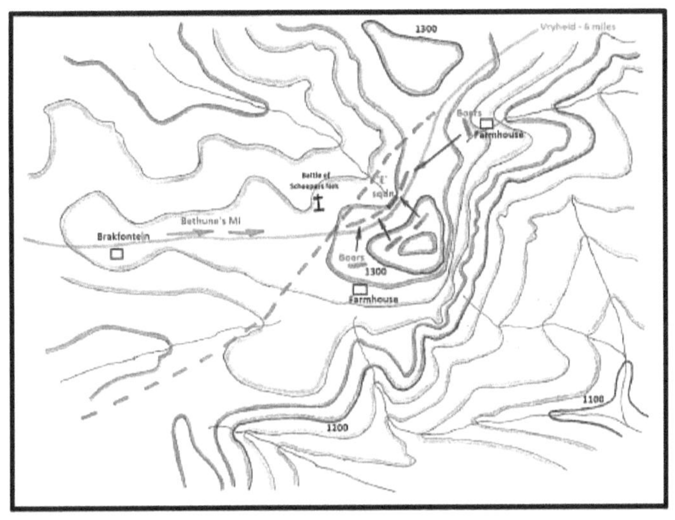

Survey map

All photos are by courtesy of the S.A. Military History Society.

One man who fought at SN surviving to fight another
day was a Swede, one Bror Emil Hjalmar Enstrom,
enlisted with Bethune's merry men 10/11/99 as No
289 Trooper Harry Enstron on the Nominal Roll.

This adventurer - tough as Swedish pine - was floored
by bullet injuries to chest, shoulder and buttocks (!?),
subsequently taken prisoner, and a few weeks later
returned to the Brits (Times newspaper reporting
prisoners handed back under flag of truce 21/7/00).

Following some care a General Hospital in Howick
Trooper 289 was sent - via SS Formosa - to Woolwich
hospital and admitted there 17/1/01.

But this worthy was made of stern stuff - after
discharge from the force 29/7/01 as permanently
disabled, he returned to SA, married Hilda Kanjila Von
Breda on 2/7/04 and - lived happily ever after - but
that is, of course, another story!

Article written in AngloBoerWar,com

Of interest Dominee Edwin Cheers Anderson, passed away
on August 12, 1947, and was buried in Ceres in the Western
Cape. His first wife, Annie Elizabeth Brink died in 1904 and
was buried in the Vryheid Cemetery. They had four children.
His second wife Johanna Petronella Kloppers, who died on
June 4, 1972 was buried with her husband in the same grave
in Ceres.

Lieutenant General Sir Edward Cecil Bethune was born on June 23, 1855 in Kensington, London, and died on November 2, 1930. He was married to Mary Lilian Elliott Lochhart.

One Hundred and Eighteen Years Later

Thieving treasure seekers dug a trench under the Scheeper's Nek monument in search of relics from the battle and, in the process, caused the large pyramid structure to topple over. Luckily with the help of the Commonwealth War Graves Commission it could be restored. A few years later there was an attempt to remove the copper plaque from the monument containing the details of those who fell at Scheeper's Nek. It has since been removed to a place of safety and replaced by a, just as beautiful, granite plaque.

Monument: Scheeper's Nek

Fitting the new granite plaque.

Scheeper's Nek 1995: some items picked up on the battle site: a piece of a whisky bottle, pottery shards, a complete .303 cartridge and a soda water cartridge.

A "reproduction" of a memorial stone which stands in the President Brand Cemetery in Bloemfontein. This stone is in remembrance of Kenneth, Ernest and Alastair Hamilton, who were the three sons of Major Bramston Hamilton. Private Kenneth Hamilton was killed in action of May 16, 1900. Private Ernest Hamilton was killed in action on May 20, 1900, at Scheeper's Nek and Private Alistair Hamilton was struck by lightning on December 1902 and was buried in the Machadodorp Military cemetery.

Photos courtesy of the South African Military History Society.

Post Anglo Boer War – A New Life

A strong woman accepts the war she went through,
And is ennobled by her scars.
Carly Simon

Hilda Kangela van Breda

Hilda Kangela van Breda at 18 years old

After being discharged from hospital in England, Harry returned to South Africa where he married Hilda Kangela (Kangela "to watch" in Zulu) van Breda in Durban, Natal, South Africa on July 2, 1904. Hilda Kangela van Breda was born in Pretoria on May 31, 1877 to Hendrik Willem van Breda and Sara Susanna Ziervogel. She died from breast cancer in Reunion, Natal, South Africa on December 27, 1941 with her son Wallace Vivian Enstrom at her bedside.

It is thought that as the van Breda and Ziervogel ancestors were involved in the Transvaal politics, they may have come to the New Republic in Vryheid when land was given to the Boers by the Zulu King Dinzulu for defeating his enemy Sibhebhu. A new republic was proclaimed in 1884. In a photo found in a book on the Vryheid Centenary 1984, Miss van Breda is shown. Two ladies on either side of Miss van Breda are family of the Boer General, Cheers Emmett, of Irish Descent. It has been documented that many Irish men fought with the Boers against the British in the Second Anglo Boer War.

In 1901 Hilda would have been twenty-five years old and her sister, Levine, twenty-six years old. Hilda's father died when she was two years old and was therefore, brought up by her mother, Sara Susanna Ziervogel, who was of Swedish heritage. The question, therefore, is whether the van Breda Family were identified as Boers and if so, was she an Afrikaans lady meeting up with a British Soldier?

Romance and Marriage

Where there is love there is life.
Mahatma Gandhi

Harry and Hilda met whilst he was ill in a fever hospital, recuperating from infection resulting from gunshot wounds sustained in the Anglo Boer War and where Typhoid and Enteric fever were rampant. She, a nurse at the time was working in the hospital which always flew a yellow flag when fever patients were admitted.

Albeit that Harry was unemployed, he and Hilda were very much in love and married on July 2, 1904 in a Civil Service. They suffered financial hardship but managed to cope. While living in Point Road, they had two sons, Emil Leonard (also known as Len) who was born in 1905 and was christened at Addington Presbyterian Church and Eric Stanley born on January 27, 1908. Point Road (now renamed Mahatma Gandhi Road) at the time had a sandy surface and horse carts were still being used.

Point Road (now Mahatma Gandhi Road) taken in 1903
with the Bluff in the background.

It was a few years before the time that Harry was in South Africa when Mohandas Gandhi arrived in 1893 as a twenty-four-year-old lawyer. He was about to return to India when an incident occurred which forced him to reconsider, and he would take up the plight of the Indian Community. The Natal Indian Congress was formed with Gandhi as its first Secretary and in 1897 he was attacked by whites in Durban for "threatening to flood Natal with Indians". It would, however, be Gandhi who formed a stretcher bearer unit that performed with valour during the Boer War. By the late 1800s, the Indian population had grown, as large numbers of Indians were recruited to work on the sugar cane farms, and in fact the highest concentration of Indians outside of India can today be found in Natal.

In 1910 while Hilda was pregnant with her third child, the family moved to the Bluff and lived at what was known as Short's Corner. They were tenants of Polly Short who would call around to the house to collect his rent. He owned all the land known as Shortlands, extending from the bay near Fynnlands to the ocean (the back beach).

They then had a further three children, a son, Wallace Vivian who was born on June 21, 1910; John who was born on August 21, 1918 and Edith Winnifred, the only daughter. Harry and Hilda were poor, times were tough, and Len their son, recalled that Hilda, his mother, used to wash and bleach flour sacks or dye them, and then sew shorts for the boys.

At first the children used to catch the morning train from Short's Corner to West's Station and cross the bay by ferry to continue their attendance at Addington School. In the afternoon they had to walk home from the ferry at Wests as there was no train service at that time of the afternoon. Later, they went to school at the Catholic Mission in Maxwell Avenue. This was when Len, Eric, Wallace and John walked to school each day. At that time Anstey's beach was known as Mission Beach. Len and Eric attended Mansfield High for their senior years, and they had to walk from home to catch the train then the ferry across the bay to town to go to school.

Harry, Hilda and first-born son Leonard

Living on the Bluff

The war does not end when you come home.
It lives on in memories of your fellow soldiers,
Sailors, airmen and Marines who gave their lives.
It endures in the wound that is slow to heal,
The disability that isn't going away,
The dream that wakes you at night,
Or the stiffening in your spine when a car backfires down
the street.
Barack Obama

The Enstrom family lived through the development of the Bluff over many years. In the days when Harry and his family resided on the Bluff, it was a mixed community. There were the Indian fisher folk who lived in houses on stilts built out over the waters of the bay of the Fynnlands area. In the shad season they would be up as the morning sun shone brightly through the blue skies, in tee shirts, jumpers and boots they would catch boat loads of fish which were then salted and sundried on trellises of bamboo.

It was this, now forgotten fishing community, who pioneered seine-fishing and the Durban fishing industry; it was these Indian fishermen who gave Durban a taste for fish curry, sardine fever and the annual shad culture. The first Indian fishermen as far back as 1860, wallowed in the bounty of the seafood of Salisbury Island. They harvested the ground feeders such as crabs and shrimps in the marshlands and in the deeper waters caught the smaller varieties of fish, while it was the women who sold vegetables.

Taking the dinghies and rowing across to the sandbars in the bay, picnic basket packed, it was not unusual to catch dozens of tiny translucent fish, *Smelts*, which when cooked were a gastronomic delight.

The Zanzibar's, the ex-slaves from Zanzibar arrived sporadically until 1880, however, by the end of that year importation of slaves from Zanzibar came to an end. In 1899 land for Zanzibari Muslims was officially transferred to them at King's Rest. From Sormany Road to Moss Road lived a large Zulu community.

In the 1940s Bluff Road was a tree lined sand track. Mr Grey who owned Grey's Inn would take a team of oxen, on what was a footpath, from Airley Road to Brighton Beach to pull the old 1920/1930 cars up the hill enabling people to have lunch at the Hilltop Inn before driving back to Durban. As he owned a large area of the Brighton Beach area, Greys Inn Road was named after his inn.

The Bluff had many separate areas as it developed, each with its own difficulties and characteristics. On the north side was the whaling station and the smell; the south side had the oil refinery not lacking its particular smell; the centre, a swamp with malaria mosquitoes. There were times when all three were present in unpredictable proportions; then there was, the deadly snakes.

Many of the Bluff roads owe their names to the first farmers who subdivided to make the stands that are presently lived on. Some of the original farmhouses remain. For many years they had the Clover dairy with the cows as well. The Bluff had many uniquely named areas. Kings Rest where reputedly Dick King rested after crossing the bay; Kings View which later became known as Crossways after the Crossways Hotel, later renamed Ocean View.

Harry's family would in the later years enjoy a bus service; the green line route, Marine Garage to Durban; the red line route Crossways to Durban and Fynnland Beach.

Fynnland Beach was not only good for swimming and fishing, but there was always plenty of activities for the *kids*. They would engage in many races including egg and spoon races.

In an article written for the "ratepayer" Harry's son Leonard wrote:

Emil Leonard Enstrom's
Memories of his Years on the Bluff

"My first impressions of the Bluff were at the age of five in the year 1910. Our family moved from Point Road to what was known as Short's Corner. We were tenants of old Mr Polly Short who I remember used to call for his rent. He owned all the land known as Shortlands extending from the bay near Fynnland to the ocean.

In those days, we children used to catch the morning train from Short's Corner to West's Station to attend Addington School and in the afternoon, we had to walk home from the ferry at

Wests as there was no train service then. We took hours to get home as there were so many things to do, such as throwing stones at fish etc.

Ferry Across the Bay

The ferry across the bay was at that time run by the Benjamins. I also remember the Gouldings who lived at the lighthouse on the end of the Bluff and the Askews who lived in a cottage at Cave Rock where the waves on rough days would spray the house with foam.

There were two houses at Island View on the hill where the present Shell houses are built, and Henry Benjamin lived there. There were two cinnamon trees at the back of Benjamin's house — we children used to chew the bark.

We spent a lot of time swimming and fishing in Durban Bay which was clean and Sandy in those days. The water of the bay used to come right up to the railway line and at low tide you could walk over to Salisbury Island at a point approximately where the flashing beacon tower is at the Dolphin Wharf. I remember Captain Wellington who appeared to me to be a hearty and jovial gentleman. He had quite a lot of rabbits and gave me a pair. My memory of Captain Vibert was rather different, especially after he caught us playing in his boat at Fynnland.

All our mail in those days had to be collected at West's which was the nearest Post Office.

Another recollection of my early days is the metal bell which was rung at Mr Armstrong's every day at noon. This was to call the cattle home for midday milking and I usually passed his Indians carrying cans of milk along the line to West's for sale at the Point.

To Town by Rowing Boat

There were, of course, no roads in those days, only bush tracks, and the only method of cartage was by donkey cart. Old Mr Lloyd went over to town by rowing boat once a week and purchased his animal food, then landed it at Fynnland from where it was taken home by a cart, on which I managed to have many a ride. In those days there was quite a lot of game and the Armstrongs and Dick Wellington hunted at Short's Corner.

The only shop I remember is the one which was run by Mr Dabinet where the barbecue stood. Old Mr Lloyd had a shop at Torquay Avenue and the O'Connells lived at the Big Fir Tree where the Bend Store is now.

Mr and Mrs Bower lived at Kings Rest and the old jail in their grounds was a relic of the days when Mr. Bower was the Justice.

Native Kraals on the Bluff

There were lots of natives living in their kraals at the Bluff in those days and there was one just where the present sewerage pumphouse is.

At the edge of the bay resided the Indian fishermen and, in the shad season I remember they brought boatloads of fish to Fynnland, which were salted and sundried on trellises of bamboo. We boys were always after bait for fishing, so we know all the Indians there.

I remember the Old Union Whaling Station near Cave Rock and the Premier, also in later years the shark factory between the two.

There were no pubs in those days, but I remember the gentlemen managing to get down to West's Public House otherwise it had to be the Clairwood Hotel.

Captain Rice and his stepsons, the Marshs, lived where Moffatt Avenue now is.

No Corporation Water

There was no Corporation water available in those days as the only water main was at the Railway line. The only people that had Corporation water were the Bowers and the Armstrongs as far as I recollect. Everyone else depended on tanks. There was no electricity here and coal or paraffin lamps were the only means of lighting.

A startling affair occurred in my early life, when Mr Armstrong and Mr Lloyd had a bout of fisticuffs where the corner of Bluff and Donegal Roads now is, of course those roads never existed then. I enjoyed this very much but Mr Lloyd was fined three pounds which was quite a sum then.

Mr. Andrews, Editor of the Sugar Journal, used to own all the land that was later Garvies beach. His home at the corner of Boynes Road and Marine Drive was burnt down. In olden times the Seridges lived at approximately the present position of the Bluff Bowling Club, but there home was burnt down. I never met them although the brick chimney existed for a long time afterwards. At Salisbury Island was an isolation Hospital, a Tea Room and other residents living on the island.

Put the Clock Back

We boys used to put mother's clock back. All you had to do in those days was miss the train, thereby avoiding school, as there were no more trains. The Mission at Ansteys Beach and the Zanzibar Natives at the Mission at Kings Rest, existed from as early as I can remember. The Garcins lived at Ansteys on top of the hill and old Mr. Garcin met his daughters at Wentworth with donkeys to ride home from school.

The dredger "Snipes" was the first to dredge a channel at Short's Corner and reclaim some land by pumping the sand to the mangroves at

Shortlands. In later years, when they started to reclaim the land where the Shell Company now is, we had wonderful sport with fish as they seemed to like the red soil. From the cutting at Island View.

Enjoyed Life

I have not mentioned half the people who lived at and enjoyed the Bluff in those days, but we children certainly enjoyed life and found plenty to do without bioscopes etc. There was a Big Bush as we called it on the seaward side of the railway line, near the present Shell Laboratory and Office. This was a projection of land into the bay where we used to look for and find, slave beads in the sand, supposedly brought by ships which careened there in olden times".

The family have over the years added snippets about living on the Bluff. At some time, Harry and his family moved to live in Torquay Avenue- their house in later years part of the Nursery Garden in that area. In those days there was no piped water to the houses, and they had water tanks. When the water tanks ran out Hilda and the boys would have to walk to Fynnlands station to get water.

Harry and Hilda eked out a living as funds were limited. When Harry first settled on the Bluff, it was a time of hope. They kept two cows for milk and for meat they used to go hunting for bush buck, duiker, in the bush at the end of the Bluff. A springbok for dinner and fish were plentiful. The

Enstrom family were competent and efficient fishermen. Taking Sloane Road off Marine Drive was Garvies, a long stretch of sand. Not only did it provide for leisurely strolls along the magnificent, unspoiled beach and dunes which were inviting, but watching the sunrise early in the morning was quite spectacular.

They knew and had inside information as where the gullies and ledges were. It was their stomping grounds. From an incredibly early age, they had lived and fished on the Bluff. Fishing, an important component, provided survival for many over the century. It was the beach where one could watch those who were fishing, watch the boats settling in for a day's fishing or simply enjoying the pristine beaches, laying on a towel and reading a book.

The Bluff too was renowned for the famous Cave Rock, the tidal pool, and rock pools to explore. Dolphins would frolic year-round, close to the shore, and whales were often spotted in the winter months as they migrated north. The thick vegetation provided home to many monkeys and mongoose. The saying for those who lived on the Bluff: "We are rough and tough and we come from the Bluff"; and they certainly were. Children roamed free and without care, playing out all day they only returned home when the street lights came on.

Harry was apparently not working and lived on a pension during his later years. He was not a well man as he still had bullets lodged in him from the war years. Len said that he learnt to swim when his father took him and threw him into the water and said, "swim you bugger, swim" and it was either swim or drown. A drastic measure to teach one to swim, but both he and all the Enstrom boys, were exceptionally good swimmers. One thing that he did well was that Harry knew how to cook fish; he taught his daughter-in-law Edna how to cook fish the correct way.

The family were rather poor, as for many years he only received a pension from the war office which is what they had to survive on and when Harry, in later years went to visit the family in Sweden he worked his way over onboard ship to pay his fare. He did not advise his family in Sweden that he was struggling; nor did he take his wife and family with him as he could not afford to do so. Harry never shied from a hard day's work; a legacy which he has passed on to his children and ultimately their children.

Throughout the years of his life post war, Harry had nightmares not only of rats in his pillow; he would wake up screaming as he was flung across the fatally unstable deck, perched at the edge of the barge's upper deck; he always woke just in time before he plunged into the sub-zero waters where the cold would certainly kill him, even if drowning did not; many a night the barge was swept away like a cork in a rushing stream straight toward the Alaskan shoreline. The nights that he woke up in a cold sweat as he felt the pain; the shock that he had been hit by enfilading fire; he would hear the horrifically loud blasts, explosions, the loud bangs, and the repetitive hammering of the Maxim and saw the numerous muzzle flashes. Harry often relived the complete mayhem and confusion as he lay there injured in the dust listening to the screams and yells of his fellow troopers.   His horse dead laying a few metres from him. The war had left him with so much pain and mental anguish.

Sadly, Harry died on June 23, 1932 at Addington Hospital in Durban from Myocardial failure following Malaria.

The information obtained from the medical documents was taken from the original documents. Photographs were taken of the original documents held in the Military Archives in Kew in England and Rosalie will forever be indebted to Rowena Wattrus who did the research, photographed every document and so painstakingly emailed them to her over several weeks.

Rowena became quite bonded to "Our Harry" as she lovingly called him and was only too happy to oblige with the research. She felt an affiliation with Harry as she too, as a child, had lived on the Bluff in Durban and at Yellow Wood Park, Montclair. It is quite amazing what a small world we live in.

By the age of twenty-seven, Harry had experienced and had been engaged in the dangerous and hard life of a seaman. He had been shot, taken prisoner of war, and was medically discharged from the army. He was an invalid. To his family, Harry was courageous and a legend.

In later years Harry's children and grandchildren told stories about the Union Whaling Station on the Bluff. Aubrey, grandson to Harry, often told that the cousins had made regular visits to the educational whaling station. The decks stained with red whale blood and the awfully bad smells hard to endure. The thought of falling off the deck into the shark infested water was graver and more than grim. On a visit,

Rosalie stood in awe of the mere size of these whales and often wondered how it was possible to hunt down the majestic creatures. It was at the station that these enormous barnacle encrusted mammals were dissected and butchered; the product used to make soap, margarine, and cooking oils.

Aubrey often recalled how, as children, they went aboard the whaling vessels in dock, where the chef fed them. His greatest delight was being given a tin of condensed milk to eat. He always had a sweet tooth. They always knew that their grandfather had been a sailor on the whaling boats but sadly had never had the pleasure of being able to talk to him or listen to all the tales which he would have been able to tell. They never knew much about their grandfather's military service.

Harry died at age fifty-nine from cardiac failure. He would no longer be able to stand on the deck of that Brig and look up into the maze of ropes and wind filled canvas overhead. He would no longer hear the noise of the breakers and the commands of the captain, feel the terrible anxiety, and fatigue or experience the days when sailors earned calloused hands and sun bronzed backs. He would never again feel the pain; the shock that he had been hit by enfilading fire; nor would he ever hear the distressingly loud blasts, explosions, loud bangs, and the repetitive hammering of the Maxim.

Harry would, however, have been proud of his descendants as most of the family had become seamen in their own right, and certainly were good and well-known fishermen. They were left a legacy where the happy times, the fair winds, the ocean, the waves, the seashells, and toes in the sand had grounded their souls.

Hilda & Vinnie von Breda

Hilda remarried after the death of Harry. Her husband was Alfred Clements; they lived at 19 East Street, Overport Durban. She later moved to Reunion.

Hilda with her son Wallace Vivian Enstrom

The van Breda Ancestors

You may choose to look the other way
But you can never say again
That you did not know.
William Wilberforce

The paternal family of Hilda van Breda (a Dutch name which originated in the Netherlands) were very prominent in the early formation of the Cape in South Africa.

Hendrik Willem van Breda

Hendrik Willem van Breda was born in the Cape, South Africa. He was the son of Dirk Gysbert van Reenen van Breda and Susanna Hendrina Wilhelmina Meyer. He was baptised in Cape Town on October 22, 1848 and died on March 10, 1878 at the age of thirty years. He married Johanna Wilhemina Roos, who was the daughter of Johannes Anthony Roos and Maria Florentina Jacobs Volsteed on Thursday, October 7, 1869 in Cape Town. She died at 50 Bree Street, Cape Town on July 1, 1873 at the age of twenty-two years. They had no children.

He married Sara Susanna Ziervogel and they had three children, Lavinia, (1875), Hendrik (1876-1947) and Hilda (1877–1941). Sara Susanna was born in Graaff -Reinet, Eastern Cape, on September 11, 1853 to Carl Frederick Ziervogel and Anna Elizabeth Ritchie. She died at home in Church Square, Vryheid on November 5, 1902 at the age of 49 years. After the death of her husband, she remarried Thomas Henry Brown who had a farm in the Greytown area.

The Ancestral Line of Hendrik van Breda

Father of Hilda Kangela van Breda

Pieter van Breda - Progenitor

Pieter van Breda was born in 1696 in Sas Van Gent, Zeeland, Netherlands. He was the son of Dirk van Breda who was born in 1666 and Maria Canaria who was born in 1670. He married Catharina Smuts (daughter of Michiel Cornelis Smuts and Cornelia Eenmaal), on August 17, 1721 in Cape Town.

Catharina Smuts died on June 30, 1781 in Cape Town.

Pieter van Breda was a soldier in the VOC (Verenigde Oostindische Compangnie) service at nine gulden per month. He arrived in the Cape July 19, 1719 in the ship *Spiering,* free burgher 1721, tailor. He bought Oranje Zigt on December 19, 1731 from Johannes Strydom a fruit and vegetable farmer for the sum of two thousand gulden which his family owned for almost two centuries. Pieter died at Oranje Zigt, now an affluent residential suburb on the slopes of Table Mountain above Reservoir, which was probably so called because either, it overlooked the orange stronghold of the Castle, and the sight of the abundant orange trees growing in Table Valley in 1759, as did his wife Catherina.

Pieter van Breda and Catherina Smuts had one son and one daughter.

Michiel van Breda

Michiel van Breda was the son of Pieter van Breda and Catharina Smuts. Michiel married Wilhelmina De Kock, daughter of Servaas de Kock and Susanna van Booyen on October 23, 1746 in Cape Town. She died on June 24, 1776 in Cape Town. He died on July 17, 1777 at Oranje Zigt. They had one child, Pieter van Breda.

Michiel van Breda was a Member of Burger Council.

Pieter van Breda

Pieter van Breda was the son of Michiel van Breda and Wilhelmina De Kock. He was baptised in Cape Town on March 1, 1750 and died on June 3, 1804.

He married Hilletje Hillegonda Smuts on Monday August 30, 1802. She was the daughter of Marthinus Smuts and Aletta Gertruida Mostert. She was baptised on April 13, 1749.

Pieter married Catharina Sophia Myburg on Sunday November 27, 1774 in Cape Town. They had two sons and two daughters. Michiel (1775-1847) was the first child and son.

Pieter married Margaretha Wilhelmina Michielse on Sunday August 14, 1803 in Cape Town. She was the daughter of Johann Adam Michielse and Johanna Elisabeth du Preez. She was baptised on June 21, 1767. They have no known children.

Michiel van Breda

Michiel van Breda (25.9.1775 – 12.8.1847)
President of Burgher Senate, Member of the first
Legislative Council,
First Mayor of Cape Town,
Farmer Oranje Zigt and Zoetendalsvallei, Bredasdorp.
Bredasdorp named after him in 1838.
Cape Town Archives Repository: M 178 Engraving by
W Geller
Photo provided by Johan van Breda

Michiel van Breda was born on September 25, 1775, baptised in Stellenbosch, Western Cape, South Africa on October 1, 1775, and died on August 12, 1847 at the age of seventy-one years.

Michiel married Catharina Gesina (Geesje) van Reenen on Sunday, December 29, 1799 in Cape Town. She was baptised on March 16, 1783. She died on July 1, 1819. They had four sons. Dirk Gysbert was the second child. (1803-1870).

Michiel then married Beatrix Elizabeth Lategan on Tuesday July 25, 1820. She was the daughter of Willem Lategan and Wilhelmina Josina Smalberger. She was baptised in February 1790 and died on July 5, 1835. They had one son.

Michiel then married Maria Adriana Smalberger, the daughter of Johan Wilhelm Smalberger and Johanna Martina Mostert on Tuesday February 24, 1837 in Swellendam, Western Cape South Africa. They have no known children.

Michiel van Breda was the President of Burgher Senate, First Mayor of Cape Town, member of the Legislative Council, farmer Oranje Zigt and Zoetendalsvallei, Bredasdorp. Bredasdorp was named after him in 1838.

Sadly, his two sons did not inherit their father's good nature and were known for their violent and uncontrollable tempers. They were socialites given to heavy drinking and abusive behaviour towards slaves and even their own wives and often clashed with the law. Barely six months after their father's death they both killed their wives. Despite the wealth and gaiety, hosting of dinner dances and hunting parties, it was not a happy family.

Dirk Gysbert van Reenen van Breda

Dirk Gysbert van Reenen van Breda was born on Thursday, May 5, 1803. He was the son of Michiel van Breda and Catharina Gesina (Geesje) van Reenen. He was baptised on July 31, 1803. He married Susanna Hendrina Wilhelmina Meyer (second cousin). He was a member of the Legislative Council. He died at Oranje Zigt, Cape Town on November 14, 1870 at the age of sixty-seven years.

At the age of twenty-five years, Dirk Gysbert van Reenen married Susanna Hendrina Wilhelmina Meyer on Tuesday, September 9, 1828 in Cape Town when she was nineteen years old. She was born on Friday September 1, 1809. She was the daughter of Gerrit Hendrik Meyer and Martha van Breda. She was baptised in Cape Town on September 10, 1809 and died on December 15, 1887 at the age of seventy-eight years. They had one son, Hendrik (1848-1878).

In the late 1860's Ratelrivier farm was bought by Dirk Gysbert van Reenen van Breda, the second son of Michiel van Breda. Michiel's wife was the daughter of Dirk Gysbert van Reenen, well known brewer, businessman and freethinking farmer. He was also a member of the Legislative Council of the Cape Colony's first elected parliament and a Cape Town municipal commissioner.

Bredasdorp

Bredasdorp the hub of the Southern Overberg, was built on the farm *Lange Fontein* but also had its fair share of neighbourly power struggles which started at a meeting to discuss the possibility of establishing a church community. With half of the delegates favouring this farm, the others opted for the farm next door *Klippedrift* which resulted in the splitting into two separate towns, *Bredasdorp* and *Napier*.

In 1837, the government bought the farm *Lange Fontein* and on May 16, 1838 the part which was to become *Bredasdorp* (South Africa's first *dorp*) was sold. Michiel van Breda, later the first Mayor of Cape Town, became instrumental in this venture as it was on his farm.

Progressively expanding their assets was a policy the van Breda family continued to follow until the largest part of Table Valley, two hundred and thirteen-morgen in the eighteenth century was acquired. Their main income came from the sale of vegetables and fruit.

They were known for their great hospitality and many significant visitors were entertained on the estate on an extravagant scale. Pieter had his own house orchestra of thirty flute players in uniform who performed in one of the many gardens, on a raised bandstand.

The Oranje Zigt house was unique in that it was a double storey, wood-floor balcony in six columns. Inside were large cool rooms with large windows, superb furnishings and an antique collector's paradise. Seven steps led from the paved pathway to the *stoep,* or veranda, entrance to the house, tier after tier of terraced fields with stonework fronts stretched towards the mountain. In front of the house was a fishpond surrounded by a cobbled courtyard. There were also two slave bells, the main one hanging suspended between two pillars. These rang at set hours or in the case of an emergency.

On sale days the bell sounded, and a flag was hoisted, the signal for ship's officers, burghers and children to proceed on their way to the estate to meander through the spacious gardens and fill their baskets with fruit and vegetables. Produce was then brought to a tree in the cobbled yard where it was weighed from an oak tree. With exotic flowers adding colour and kilometres of shady walks along the way was a pleasurable occasion for all.

The demise of Oranje Zigt started in 1877 when, in spite of being entailed, the Purchase Act enabled the Municipality to buy more that twelve-morgen, on which to construct water reservoirs. Five years later they released further portions of the estate and the municipality also acquired rights to seize the many springs on the estate. Without water the farm became quite useless.

Members of the family continued to live there well into the twentieth century, but gradually more were sold until ultimately there was little left except the double-story house in Sidmouth Avenue. It is an authentic museum since the van Breda family bought lovely furniture, silverware, and art treasures into their home. The house was eventually also purchased by the City Council in 1947 allegedly to become a community museum. However, in August 1947, two hundred and eighty-seven antiques were auctioned and on April 1, 1955 the house was demolished to make way for a sports club and lawns. Now only the name of the suburb remains in the van Breda possessions.

What takes some getting used to today and which is horrifying was the fact that the van Breda family were slave owners and although it is easy to judge people who lived long ago according to the values that we believe in today; one must remember that the world looked quite different in the days of chattel slavery at the Cape. The concept of human rights and democracy as we know them today did not exist then. In those days people had different ideas of justice too. It was accepted that a person accused of committing a crime could be tortured to obtain a confession. What must be realised is that the Cape where the van Breda families lived, was colonised by the Dutch East India Company; or the VOC (Verenigde Oostindische Compangnie). All rules, laws and decisions taken by the government were aimed at increasing the profits of the VOC. The welfare of people was less important, therefore, having a cheap and submissive labour force fitted into the plans of the VOC. (Iziko Museums of Cape Town).

It is easy to judge people who lived long ago according to the values that we believe in today. One must remember that the world looked very different in the days of chattel slavery at the Cape.

Today, Bredasdorp is a sleepy agricultural town amid a peaceful landscape of sheep farms and wheatfields at the southern most region of Africa. It is clean and pleasantly situated on the slopes of a 368-metre-high hill called the Preekstoel (pulpit) on the ridges of which grow a profusion of giant proteas. Wheat, wool and wildflowers, are the principal products of the Bredasdorp district.

Pride of place at the entrance of Bredasdorp is a life size statue of a merino sheep which stands at the gates of the Farmer's Co-op on Swellendam Road and which honours the sheep which brought prosperity to the district. The route crosses a region well known for its influence on the South African wool trade. Michiel van Breda, regarded as the father of the merino sheep industry, saw the potential of raising Merino sheep on his farm Zoetendalsvallei, named after the ship Zoetendaal which was shipwrecked along the Cape Agulhas coast, and that kickstarted the now established local wool trade.

The Ziervogel Ancestors

The maternal ancestors of Hilda van Breda, the Ziervogels, were originally from Sweden and were a very educated and accomplished family. Sara Ziervogel (Hilda's Mother) was the daughter of Carl Frederick Ziervogel and Anna Elizabeth Ritchie. Carl being the son of Jeremias Frederick Ziervogel, a prominent Graaff-Reinet citizen and member of the Cape Legislative Assembly between 1854-1873. (Boksburg Historical Association – April 2008 Newsletter)

Stephanus Ziervogel, son of Johannes Ziervogel and seventh Great Grandfather of Hilda, was born on March 9, 1570 and died on January 26, 1623. His burial took place at the Evangelical Church, Helbra, Nr Mansfield, Saxony, Prussia, Germany. In the Evangelical country, at the Helbra Church is a tombstone with a long epitaph which says that among other things:

> *Here is the place of rest of Stephanus Ziervogel, Country Judge and Inspector of Mines, born on the 9th March 1570 and died on the 26th January 1623 in the age of 52 years.*

The position in the churchyard of the Evangelical Church of Germany, Helbra, was in contrast to the others in that it faces the north. Far and wide the tomb is known as the *Swedish Tomb*. Stephanus Ziervogel was buried facing north to Sweden due to his grief on the departure to Sweden of his favourite grandson Samuel Ziervogel.

Samuel was born on September 16, 1616 in Eisleben Mansfield, Province of Saxony, Germany and died on January 29, 1672 in Stockholm, Tyska, Sweden. He was a pharmacist at Halle, Leipzig and Dresden. In 1647 he was appointed pharmacist to the dowager queen Maria Eleonora of Sweden while she resided in Stettin and followed her in 1648 to Sweden. After her death in 1655 he took over the pharmacy *The Swan* in Stockholm from Casper Schps and at the time of his death he was recorded as being the Pharmacist to the Swedish Court.

Ewald Benedictus Ziervogel third Great Grandfather to Hilda, was born on September 23, 1728 in Stockholm and died on June 13, 1765 in Uppsala. His occupation was Author and Librarian at Royal Academy, Uppsala, Librarian at University of Uppsala, Sweden and famous coin collector. He was a professor at the University of Uppsala and amongst other things he made a map of the whole of the world.

Ewald Ziervogel married Anna Christina Hultman and they had five children:

     I.   Elizabeth Brigitta Christina;

     II.   Samuel Frederik "Ziererik";

     III.   Carel Ewald;

     IV.   Aegidius Benedictus; and

     V.   Christina Juliana "Ulrica".

According to tradition Carel Ewald Ziervogel and Aegidius Benedictus Ziervogel, third great uncles of Hilda van Breda were the founders of the Ziervogel family in South Africa. They came to the Cape of Good Hope in 1777 after having learnt business methods in Sweden.

The Ziervogel family lobbied the Transvaal Government extensively for official appointments and soon became well known in the South African Republic. Thomas Ritchie Ziervogel (uncle to Hilda) was court messenger in the Zoutpansberg in 1879 and after resigning this position he sought appointment as Landdrost Clerk at Christiana. Sara Suzanna Ziervogel was the mother to Hilda.

Carl Frederick Ziervogel, (grandfather to Hilda), trekked with his stock to the Transvaal approximately in 1873. Thomas Burger, then President of the Transvaal appointed Carl as Magistrate for Zoutpansberg and westerly districts in 1875. He hired a farm *Upsala* which was called *Opsaal* by the Boers – later renamed Sterkloop, where Pietersburg now stands. Carl left there and bought a farm on the Reef, then sold it to buy what became Meintjies Kop where the Union Buildings were later built. There is still a Ziervogel Street in Arcadia. As magistrate he had to hold court in Eerstegoud regularly and once a month at the foot of the Zoutpansberg. He bought the farm Leeuwpoort in 1860 where Boksburg was later established. He was President of the Agricultural Society and was Landdrost to Pretoria from 1882 – 1886.

According to the *Boksburg Historical Association – April 2008 Newsletter* in "1886 gold was found on Carl Frederick Ziervogel's farm, Leeuwport. So began the Goldfield from which Boksburg emerged."

Anna Susanna Ziervogel (third Great Grandmother to Aubrey Enstrom) is also a first cousin to Dietlof Siegfried Marè, the Grandfather of Carolina Augusta van Heerden married to Johannes Alexander Osmers, Grand Uncle to Rosalie.

War, Peace and Prosperity

Never think that war, no matter how necessary,
Not how justified, is not a crime.
Ernest Hemmingway

World War II

On September 1, 1939 Germany invaded Poland without warning. The evening of September 3, 1939 Britain and France were at war with Germany and within a week Australia, New Zealand, Canada and South Africa had also joined the war.

Sweden remained officially neutral during World War II, although its neutrality has been vigorously debated. Sweden was under German influence for most of the war, as ties to the rest of the world were cut off through blockades and Sweden.

Emil Leonard Enstrom

Emil Leonard Enstrom: Airman (Carpenter) No. 337476, South African Air Force, enlisted on March 30, 1942 in Durban. He was based in Durban at Congella.

He was discharged on March 31, 1946.

His Medals were:

The War Medal 1939/45 Serial 8629 Desp. 9-7-58

Africa Service Medal Re No. 41/8872 Book 18 Page 83.

Emil Leonard Enstrom was the firstborn child and son of Harry and Hilda. He married Edna Vivian Sharples on July 4, 1931 and they had three children. Edna died in the Cape on August 14, 1983.

Len was a carpenter by trade and built several houses for his family. At a roof wetting, the family gathered and sang "Bless this house O Lord we pray".

According to a newspaper report found in Edna's bible, Len and his brother Erik had dived into the water from the wharf to rescue an Indian lady from drowning. The report further stated that Edna had waded waist deep to assist her sons in dragging the lady out of the water to safety.

Len, as he was known, died on August 16, 1973 in Durban.

Erik Stanley Enstrom

Eric Stanley Enstrom: Private No. 7336, 2nd Battalion in the Durban Royal Light Infantry, S.A. Forces. He embarked at Durban per ss *Llandoff Castle* for the Middle East on July 20, 1941 and disembarked in the Suez on August 12, 1941.

He was listed as missing believed to have been taken Prisoner of War on November 20, 1942 which was confirmed on November 28, 1942 when it was recorded that he was captured by the Germans at Tobruk in North Africa.

He was held in Northern Italy where he died on December 29, 1942 of enterocolitis and buried at Bari War Cemetery located on the outskirts of Bari in the locality of Carbonara, Italy. His name being placed on a war memorial in Durban.

His decorations were:

1939 – 45 Star; Africa Star; The War Medal 1939 – 1945
Africa Service Medal

The site of Bari War Cemetery was chosen in November 1943. The Army Group had their headquarters in the town during the early stages of the Italian campaign and continued to be an important supply base and hospital centre, with the 98th General Hospital stationed there from October 1943 until the end of the war.

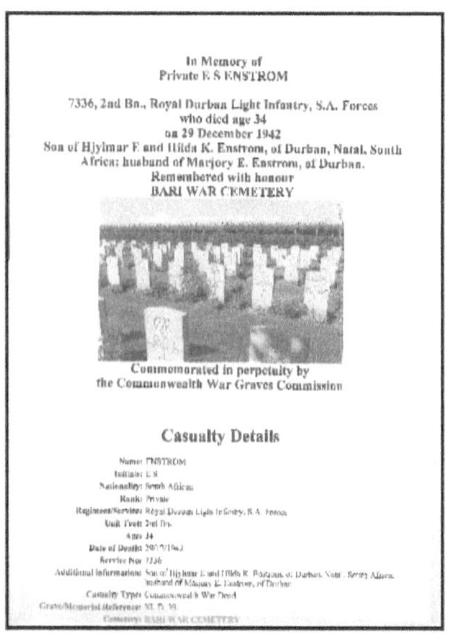

Besides garrison and hospital burials, the cemetery contains graves brought in from south-eastern Italy from the rich to the poor, as well as men who died in two disastrous explosions in the harbour of Bari, when ammunition ships exploded in December 1943 during a German air raid. The cemetery contains 2,128 Commonwealth burials of the Second World War, 170 of them unidentified.

Eric Enstrom was posted missing on June 20, 1942 having been captured at Tobruk and confirmed as a Prisoner of War on November 28, 1942. He died on December 29, 1942.

Photos which were sent home to family prior to his death.

Taken aboard the *Llandoff Castle* July 20, 1941

Egypt February 1942

Prisoner of War Camp Brindisi.

A letter from Buckingham Palace was received by the family of Eric.

The Queen and I offer you our heartfelt sympathy in your great loss.
We pray that your Country's gratitude for a life so nobly given in its service may bring you some measure of consolation.
Signed: George R.I.

Eric Stanley Enstrom who was born on January 27, 1908 married Marjory Elizabeth Sharples and they had four children.

Wallace Vivian Enstrom

The little he had he gave to others.

On March 9, 1942 Wallace Vivian Enstrom (No. 315503) took the Oath to bear true allegiance to his Majesty King George VI and signed as a volunteer member of the Union Defence Forces. He was assigned to the coast Garrison and Citizen Forces, posted to the 7th Infantry Brigade and to the

S.A. Medical Corp.

For a while he was attached to the Mobile Dental Unit as a driver. He also spent time at the Springfield Military Hospital in Durban and was finally seconded to work on the Hospital Ship "*Amra*" as a boiler assistant.

Picture of the Amra – Courtesy of John Prescott – British India Ships

Photo courtesy of John Prescott – British India Ships

The British India Ship the "*Amra*" was named after a village east of Benares. It is also the name of a flowering tree that grows at high altitudes. The "*Amra*" was launched on April 29, 1938 and sailed from London on November 18, 1938 on her delivery voyage to Calcutta to begin her brief service as a Burma mailship.

With her speed and extensive accommodation, she was soon swept into trooping duties spending two periods in 1940 as a personnel ship. On December 28, 1940 she was requisitioned as a Hospital Ship (No. 41: 385 beds, 107 Medical Staff), her first service being between Somaliland and East and South Africa.

In 1943 she moved into the Mediterranean evacuating the wounded from Sicily and Salerno landings and was under constant German attack, despite being clearly marked and illuminated. She completed service in September 1946.

Wally, as he was known, was on deck during one of the German attacks and suffered shrapnel wounds to the face. He did not leave the army at the end of the war but continued to work at the Springfield Military Hospital until 1947 where he met Sylvia Paynter who would ultimately become his second wife.

On September 3, 1944 he was awarded the Africa Service Medal.

He was discharged with efficiency and an exemplary character, of sober habits.

Wallace Vivian Enstrom was born on June 21, 1910. He married a vivacious redhead, Ethel Newman Armstrong, who was born in February 1907 in Ixopo, Natal. She was the

daughter of Harold Armstrong and Edna Rowbottom. Wally
and Ethel had two children.

John Harold Enstrom

John Harold Enstrom: 2nd Royal Durban Light Infantry
Battalion unit was captured by the Germans at Tobruk in North
Africa. He was held in Northern Italy and later returned on the
ship HMS "*Strathaird*" from Europe after the war crossing the
equator on June 6, 1945.

In September 1939, *Strathaird* and *Strathnaver* were
requisitioned as troop ships transporting troops to the Middle
East. *Strathaird* sailed on two convoys, before returning to
Liverpool to undergo a refit. However, before completion, she
was sent to Brest to evacuate 6000 civilians and troops,
returning them to Plymouth, after which the refit was
completed, and she returned to her wartime duties. Having
carried some 128,961 persons and covered 387,745 miles,
Strathaird was handed back to P & O at the end of 1946.

John embarked at Durban per ss *Llandoff Castle* on the 20
July 1941 and disembarked in the Suez on the 12 August 1941.

It was believed that he was taken prisoner of war on the 20 June 1942 which was confirmed on the 28 November 1942. He was in Prisoner of War camp 85 (3450) from 25 November 1942 and released on the 29 April 1945 when he arrived in the U.K. Two brothers, Erik and John, it appears, were in the same Infantry, both being confirmed as Prisoners of War on November 28, 1942.

Decorations were:

1939 – 1945 Star; Africa Star; The War Medal 1939 – 1945 and The Africa Service Medal.

John Harold Enstrom was born on August 21, 1918 and died in Durban in 1987. He married Maureen Beryl Kidwell who died in 1985. They had thirteen children.

Edith Richards/ Reynolds
Daughter of Harry and Hilda Enstrom

Edith was the fourth child of Harry and Hilda and the only daughter. Although she did not participate in World War II, she had two children and was employed as a post woman delivering mail throughout areas of Durban.

Rosalie Moore's Ancestors

James Moore
Grandfather of Rosalie Enstrom (nee Moore)

James Moore on the farm at Ferndale Transvaal

James Moore was born about June 1879 in Belfast, Antrim, Ireland. He died on September 27, 1941 in Algemene Hospital, Johannesburg. He married Sarah Caroline van Zyl. They lived in Ferndale, Transvaal.

James Moore and Sarah van Zyl had six children:

    I.   Joseph James Moore was born on November 14, 1915. He died in April 1982 in Durban. He married Johanna Wilhelmina Faderl, daughter of Michael Faderl and Johanna Wilhelmina Osmers on April 18, 1938 in Durban. She was born on August 25, 1922 in Durban and died on February 25, 1999 in Welkom, South Africa;

    II.   John Charles Moore was born on September 17, 1920. He married Joyce;

    III.   Edward Macfay Henry Moore;

IV.   Colleen Jeanette Moore. She married George
       Izat;
V.   Annie Isabella Moore. She married James
       Henry Stafford;
VI.   Elizabeth Sophia Moore. She married
       Frederick James Mitchell.

James Moore served in World War 1 in the South African Expeditionary Forces as Private No. 1397 in the 7th Regiment of the South African Infantry. He enlisted at the age of 35 and took the "Oath to be taken by the Recruit on Attestation" on the 1 December 1915 at Potchefstroom whereby he swore to be faithful and bear true allegiance to His Majesty King George the Fifth. At the time his address was shown as 18 Park Street, Jeppe, Johannesburg.

His description on Enlistment was shown as being thirty-five years of age. (To be determined according to the instruction given in the Regulations for Army Medical Services). His height was five feet ten and a half inches. Chest measurement, minimum thirty-five inches, maximum expansion thirty-nine inches. He had a fresh complexion, blue eyes, and brown hair. Religion shown as Presbyterian.

He departed on ss *Prof. Woermann* for the Middle East on January 22, 1916.

On February 12, 1916 he was dangerously wounded in action having been shot through the chest at Salaita Hill East Africa, whilst on active service. The battle took place as part of the three-pronged offensive into German East Africa launched by General Jan Smuts, who had been given overall command of the Allied forces in the region.

Salaita Hill was a strategic lookout post close to the border town of Taveta and with its proximity to the border with German East Africa, and the fact it was thought to be defended by a small detachment of just three hundred men without artillery also marked it out as an initial objective for Smuts' offensive. In preparing for the forthcoming advance into German East Africa, the British took up the defensive position on Salaita Hill and on February 12, 1916 under the British commander, Brigadier-General Malleson, (who had little combat experience, having served on the staff of Field Marshall Kitchener, and as part of the British military mission to Afghanistan prior to the outbreak of the First World War....) they advanced to attack Salaita.

The British 1st East African Brigade advancing in line from the east towards Salaita Hill, the mounted Infantry Company secured the left (southern), 2nd Rhodesia Regiment were on the left whilst the 2nd Loyal North Lancashires were in the centre and 130th Baluchis were on the right. To the north and moving independently the 2nd South African Infantry Brigade under Brigadier-General P.S. Beves who deployed to make a right attack, with 5th South African Infantry on the left, 7th South African Infantry in the centre and 6th South African Infantry on the right.

Supporting fire was provided by the Indian Volunteer Maxim Gun Company, four RNAS armoured cars, 28th Mountain Battery, No. 1 Light Battery (Logan's), Calcutta Volunteer Battery, No. 3 and No. 4 Heavy Battery. The British artillery pounded the hill but expended their ammunition on unoccupied German positions due to incorrect intelligence. The German secondary trenches at the summit of Salaita Hill were targeted instead of the front line, which was further down the slope. The barrage therefore alerted the defenders to the coming attack without disrupting their ability to oppose it. The 1st East African Brigade halted about noon 1,000 yards east of the hill at the edge of the cleared ground which German machine guns were dominating.

The 2nd South African Infantry Brigade was in its first action and the soldiers struggled to cope with a hot sun, thick bush and thirst. The 7th South African Infantry got to within 500 yards of the hill but began taking casualties, 6th South African Infantry to the north were ordered to continue advancing, and 5th South African Infantry were deployed in reserve. Belfield's Scouts lost contact with the infantry.

The 15 Field Company then suddenly counter-attacked the 6th South African Infantry and Brigadier-General Beves sent 5th South African Infantry to secure the northern flank. The German, Abteilung Schulz (6, 9 and 24 Field Companies) had been swiftly marching towards the sound of the guns from the west, and as it rounded the north end of the hill it immediately counter-attacked the 5th and 6th South African Infantry. The exhausted and disorientated South Africans now suddenly saw six hundred Askari with bayonets fixed charging down on them screaming:

"Piga! Piga!" (Shoot! Shoot!).

The South Africans mostly broke and bolted back towards their start line. Some platoons of the 7th South African Infantry ran south into the 1st East African Brigade's area.

The 2nd SA Infantry Brigade suffered 138 casualties (30 men were missing and were never seen again). The 2nd Rhodesia Regiment suffered five men slightly wounded, three men severely wounded, and lost three men killed: viz:

      I.   1087 Sergeant Arthur Roland Carter (ex-BSAP);

      II.   1212 Private Robert Cran Jamieson; and

      III.   1010 Private Oswald Puckle.

All three are buried in Taveta CWGC Cemetery, Kenya.

James Moore was transferred on February 13, 1916 to the Base Hospital, E.A.E.F. M'bulfuni, at Voi, East Africa and was invalided per *H.S. Ebani* arriving at Cape Town on April 2, 1916 being transferred to the Military Hospital at Wynberg. He was discharged from hospital on April 13, 1916. He was discharged from the army as medically unfit at Wynberg on August 11, 1916.

There were several instances which occurred whilst on active service, viz;

      I.   When on active service he broke out of hospital on the 27 July 1916;

      II.   Drunk;

      III.   When in confinement attempting to escape;

      IV.   Using violence to a person in whose custody he was placed. Forfeits 5 days' pay for absence, RW 6 days CB and to forfeit six days pay. (Ref

OR100/1. Ex a/36. H/R.) (Ref. Gen Dep. Ord. No. 97.98.16)

His address on discharge was 113 Rand Road, Germiston, Transvaal. His pension per week was 12/6d with allowance per week to each of three children. 1/3 Pension per annum at the rate of Thirty pounds under Act 29 of 1916. Both, for twelve months, subject to re-medical examination from 12 August 1916. His pension was renewed to 13/9d from 11 August 1917, allowance three children per week 6/3d September 3, 1917. Pension per week one pound, seventeen shillings and six pence less p. paid from April 1, 1918 to December 31, 1918.

James Moore was Awarded the King Certificate 3156 and Silver War Badge No. 3158.

On his death he was accorded a Military Funeral.

Joseph James Moore
Father of Rosalie Angeline Enstrom (nee Moore)
Father-in-law of Aubrey Enstrom

Joseph James Moore (No. 201553) took his Oath of Allegiance to his Majesty King George VI on July 5, 1940 and signed as a volunteer of the Union Defence Forces. He was assigned to the South African Engineers Corp as he was a Stonemason by trade.

On March 10, 1941 he was promoted to Lance Corporal. His rate of pay went from 7/- a day (70c) to 11/- (one dollar ten cents) a day.

He embarked for the Middle East on June 6, 1941 per "*ss Nova Scotia*" ER318.

The *Nova Scotia* – Warren Line – made her maiden voyage in May 1926 from Liverpool to St. Johns NF, Halifax, Boston.

In 1941 she was requisitioned as a troopship and on December 4, 1942 while sailing from Aden to Durban with 127 crew, 12 service personnel, 6 non-military passengers and 780 Italian Prisoners of War under the guard of 130 South

African Troops was torpedoed by a German submarine. She sank off the Coast near Lourenco Marques (position 28.30S 33.00 E) and sank rapidly with heavy loss of life. The total death toll was reported as 863 which made it one of Britain's worst maritime disasters of war. (wartime disasters at sea by David Williams)

During Joe's service he was hospitalised on a few occasions with Bronchitis and Synovitis. It would appear that this resulted in surgery to his left knee.

He was finally discharged on November 29, 1945 which by then, he had been promoted to Corporal, his decorations being:

1939 – 1945 Star; Africa Star; Defence Medal (British);

The War Medal 1939 – 1945; Africa Service Medal;

8th Army Clasp

Serial 4851 Desp. 23/1/54, Reg. 0424 Book 9 Page?

John Charles Moore

Joseph James & brother John Charles Moore

John Charles Moore (No. 75847) (brother of Joseph James Moore) took his Oath of Allegiance to his Majesty King George VI on June 28, 1940 and signed as a volunteer of the Union Defence Forces. He was assigned to the 1st Pretoria Highlands Corp. John like his brother, (Joseph also known as Joe) too was recorded as being a Stonemason.

On December 9, 1940 was promoted to Class "A" Stonemason and his rate of pay was increased from 8/- per day to 9/- per day.

He embarked from Durban for Mombasa on February 27, 1941 per *"ss Eclandia"* with the 9th field Coy. S.A.E.C. (E.R.233) and disembarked on March 4, 1941. On December 23, 1941 he returned to the Union of S.A. per *ss Dilivara* arriving on January 6, 1942.

On August 9, 1943 he embarked at Durban per *ss Burina* and disembarked in the Suez on September 1, 1943 and was posted to the 13th Field Coy. S.A.E.C. On February 23, 1944 he was admitted to hospital and discharged on February 29, 1944.

During John's service he was hospitalised on a few occasions and in fact spent six weeks in the Springfield Hospital in Durban from September 27, 1942 being discharged on November 5, 1942. He completed a Trade Test on December 7, 1943 and his rate of pay was increased to 10/- per day. He was finally discharged on December 5, 1945 his decorations being:

1939 – 1945 Star; Africa Star; Italy Star; The War Medal 1939 – 1945; Africa Service Medal.

World War II was of six years duration, they were long and bloody years of total war fought over many thousand square kilometres. It involved every major world power in a war for global domination resulting in more than 60 million people losing their lives and most of Europe and part of Asia lying in ruins. (World War – 2.net)

Michael Faderl

Grandfather of Rosalie Enstrom (nee Moore)

Michael Faderl was born in Germany in about 1896. He died on August 2, 1962 in Durban. He married Johanna Wilhelmina Osmers, who was born on June 21, 1895 in King William's Town, Eastern Cape and who died on November 11, 1966 in Durban. They had three daughters:

I.   Hilda Mary Faderl. Born May 29, 1914. She died on January 13, 1997 in Durban;

II. Ann Mathilda Faderl. Born June 22, 1916. She married Kenneth N Jack;

III. Johanna Wilhelmina Faderl. Born on August 25, 1922 in Durban. She died February 25, 1999 in Welkom, South Africa.

Michael Faderl was the son of Ignatz Faderl and Anna Maria Bogner. Both were born in Rosenheim Gemeindefreies Gebiet, Oberbayern, Bavaria Germany.

Anna (Muta) Bogner departed Germany on February 25, 1903 with her three children. Ignatz (Fata) Faderl had left Germany some time before.

Anna's residence was shown as Ubersel. They sailed on the ship *Konig,* Dutch East Africa Line from Hamburg as immigrants and travelled third class. Ports of arrival: Bremerhaven, Amsterdam, Lissabon, Las Palmas, South Africa. (Vol. 373-7 1, V111 A 1 Band 140 Page 391.)

Ignatz Faderl and Anna Maria Bogner had three children:

    I. Michael Faderl;

    II. Ignatz Faderl; and

    III. Maria Faderl.

Julius William Osmers
Patriarch of the Osmers Family in South Africa
Maternal Great Grandfather of Rosalie Enstrom (nee Moore)

Julius William Osmers

Julius William Osmers, first son and third child born to John Carsten Osmers and Johanne Sophie Schwitz. He was born on July 27, 1870 in Bremen, Germany, emigrated on November 19, 1893 from Bremen, Germany and arrived on December 28, 1893 in South Africa on the vessel *Cattendijk*. He died on 5 September 1930.

After having three bans called, he married Marie Mathilde Birkholz on October 23, 1894 by P Plegenberg in the German Baptist Church, Bethany, King Williamstown, South Africa, witnessed by F Groenewald and H Grapentin.

Julius William Osmers and Marie Mathilde Birkholz had ten children in 23 years.

He moved to East London until 1910 then moved to Garsfontein, Pretoria. While Julius lived in Garsfontein, he was a horticulturist and designed and planted the gardens in Burgers Park and the Union Buildings.

He was also a great artist and very talented. He painted the Transvaal Coat of Arms, the official heraldic symbol of the South African Republic from 1866 to 1877 and later from 1881 to 1902, in Paul Kruger House.

Some of his paintings are also in the museum in Boom Street in Pretoria. When General Joubert's wife died, Julius took all the telegrams of condolences and sympathy and re-wrote them in his handwriting with his signature. These were later framed.

Julius Osmers later relocated to the Lowfeld, Tzaneen in 1924 where he was responsible for the planning and the establishing of the orange orchards at Letaba Estates. His wife

Marie Mathilde Osmers became matron at the girls boarding house of Letaba Estates, situated on the Letaba River, Limpopo District. Girls from afar came to Letaba to work as orange pickers. It was during WW II that Johanna Wilhelmina Faderl Moore (mother to Rosalie Enstrom) worked in this orchard packing oranges.

In Search of Freedom and Opportunity

"No bird soars too high if he soars with his own wings."
William Blake

Aubrey Allen Enstrom
Pioneer of the Enstrom Family
in Australia

Aubrey and his wife Rosalie

Aubrey Allen Enstrom was the second born child and son of Wallace Vivian Enstrom and Ethel Newman Armstrong. He was born on January 8, 1937 at Addington Hospital in Durban, South Africa. He married Rosalie Angeline Moore, at St. Joseph's Catholic Church, Stamford Hill Road, Durban on March 23, 1957.

Aubrey Allen Enstrom died on June 7, 2018 in the Caboolture Hospital and was buried on June 14, 2018 at the Beerwah Cemetery. Rosalie Angeline Moore was born on September 11, 1938. They had five children:

I.   Jennifer Rose Enstrom – born in the Salvation Army Mothers' Hospital, Greyville, Durban on October 12, 1957 and died on October 18, 1957. She is buried in Stellawood Cemetery in Durban:

II.   Gary Patrick Enstrom – born November 9, 1958:

III.   Mark Aubrey Enstrom – born June 25, 1960:

IV.   Kerry Leigh Enstrom – born June 27, 1967:

V.   Susan Clare Enstrom– born June 15, 1969:

Aubrey the Early Years

Aubrey was born at Addington Hospital in Durban on January 8, 1937. Ethel had been admitted as she doubled over with each contraction. The pain was severe and dominated her entire being. As she lay on the bed in the labour room, the pain was clear on her face, then a gush of water.

"It is time to push" shouted the midwife.

Ethel felt sick, the sweat dripping off her face, while the nursing staff were hovering in the background. Her husband, Wally, was pacing the highly polished linoleum floor of the corridor crammed with patient trolleys. After some time, the screams of a baby could be heard. They were loud and strong, while Ethel was feeling exhausted from the ordeal. Wally was called in and they were able to share the intimacy of a little family as the baby was placed on her chest. They kissed and cuddled this bundle of joy, a boy; there was nothing but love which exuded from the happy parents. They inspected the tiny fingernails as his miniature finger grasped Ethel's finger, the little hands, and the feet.

Two years later one could hardly imagine the trauma which the family suffered when Ethel was knocked by a truck in Mc Donald Road, Durban. She was almost in the middle of the road; she hesitated as the truck hit her. A screech of brakes, then nothing. Wally rushed to the scene and knelt by his wife.

"Someone please, call an ambulance" he shouted.

She later died in Addington Hospital with Wally, eyes blank, fatigued, and unable to grasp the events of the day, by her side. Two years prior, they were ecstatically happy as Aubrey was born into the world. Together they were going to raise their fair haired, blue eyed baby, every moment was so rich; now she was gone.

His head in his hands, Wally pondered all the small things in life, then his mind drifted back to the moment he looked out of the window, heard the screeching of brakes, the dull thud, and witnessed the accident which claimed the life of his wife. Aubrey was two years old, and his brother was four years old. What would he do? He felt alone and desolate. In the early months after the death of their mother, they were passed around among well-meaning aunts but soon a decision would be made which would change the trajectory of their young lives.

Wallace Vivian Enstrom was conscripted, and on March 9, 1942 took the Oath to bear true allegiance to his Majesty King George VI and signed as a volunteer member of the Union Defence Forces. He was assigned to the coast Garrison and Citizen Forces, posted to the 7th Infantry Brigade and to the

South African Medical Corp. Wally had to make the decision to place his two young boys in a Catholic orphanage, Nazareth House. He was heartbroken.

Wally held the hands of two small boys as they approached the two-storey building which would become home to the boys for many years. The waiting room was still, except for the tick of the old wooden clock hanging on the wall. A musty smell hung in the air while the boys fidgeted uncontrollably. Wally tried to ignore it. His face was drawn and pale. He tried to think about happier times when he walked along the bustling Durban docks stinking of dead fish and seaweed. He thought about how the waves came day and night; it was like music to the ears. Would he make it through the war? What would become of his children?

Finally, with the frightened gleam in their eyes and the hopelessness in their expressions, they were led through the heavy wooden door to their new surroundings. There were times when Aubrey suffered from a state of loneliness and despair. He was small for his five years, thick blonde hair and fair skin and he felt abandoned. Wally, on the other hand, was facing the next chapter in his life, with a sick feeling in the pit of his stomach.

Aubrey's young life was spent mostly in the orphanage. This was without doubt a significant influence on him and he had to be admired for the way he forged his own unique approach to life; a life lived on two continents and on a forty-foot yacht, cruising on the seas along the East Coast of Australia.

Despite the drawbacks, he was a happy go lucky child. After the war, the family were impoverished; he never had warm clothes or shoes. He accepted whatever life threw at him. It was his eyes of sheer mischief, his heart of gold and the cheerful smile that went all the way to his core that got him through. He enjoyed the freedom, the natural feel of grass tickling his feet, the feel of searing hot scorching sand which numbed the feet on the beach. This was what prepared him for life. The goodness within him branched out into all he did. As he grew older, the good-looking friendly face was just a reflection of the way he was.

When the war was over Wally took his sons out of the orphanage but not before he had met and married Sylvia Paynter. She was a seamstress at the Springfield Military Hospital and Wally was at the time seconded to the position of driver at the hospital.

Wally with second wife Sylvia Paynter

They then moved into the Austerity Flats at Wentworth, accommodation which was allocated to returned service men and their families. Aubrey said that things were tough, they were poor, and rations were still in place. Wally also felt that it was his duty to take care of his only sister, Edith Winifred Enstrom, and her two daughters.

Aubrey attended Fynnlands State School where he remained until he completed Standard six, equivalent to grade eight nowadays, and it was at this time too that his Father and the family joined the Full Gospel Church at Jacobs. Aubrey became very competent and proficient at knowing the Bible off by heart and received top marks at Sunday School. He also played football for Fynnlands Football Club.

Aubrey at age 14 years

When Rosalie met Wally, he was an elderly man of medium build, softly spoken, and unassuming. He was a modest man who lived his life by the "Word of God". Once a week he stood on the General Post Office steps in the centre of Durban City on a Saturday morning and along with others, Bible in hand, with great enthusiasm, until his throat was raw and dry, preached the teachings of Christ, trying to convert the non-believers. He had a gift of true evangelical and spiritual teaching. He was the most unashamed man protesting his faith and love for the God which he so worshipped and adored. Passers-by stopped, some joined in the praying, others stopped just to hear him speak, others sniggered and sneered. He lived his life as a Christian, the most generous and humbling man ever. The inscription on his grave said it all "What little he had he gave to others."

Wally loved his children unconditionally, and they returned that love. In Aubrey's darkest moments he called on his Father for help.

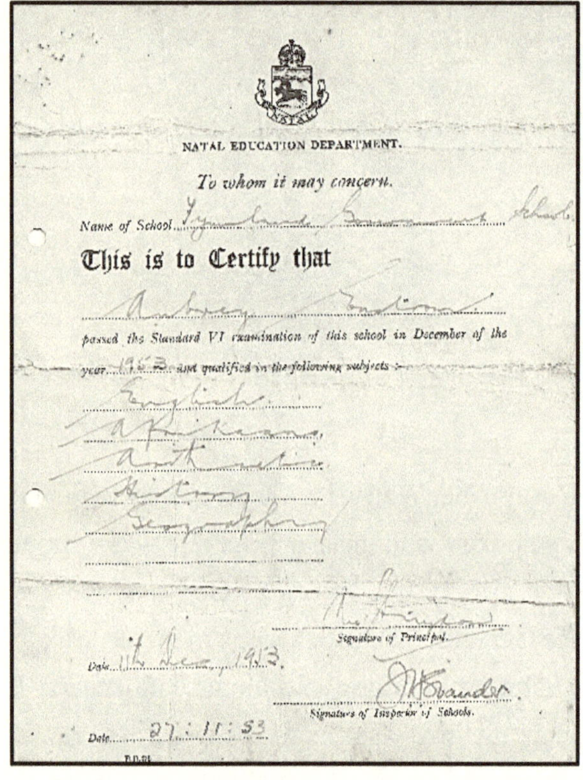

School Certificate

Once Aubrey completed school, he worked for the Durban Corporation, City Engineers Department, Old Fort Road, Durban. On commencement of service, he was employed as an Apprentice Bricklayer, Artisan Bricklayer, Temporary Clerk of Works, and Supervisor (Building and Services).

CERTIFICATE OF SERVICE

This Certificate is given without alteration or erasure of any kind.
No Certificate will be given in the case of a servant discharged for an offence of a serious nature.

CITY ENGINEER'S Department. Reference No. 5795

I Hereby Certify that AUBREY ALLAN ENSTROM. was employed in the service of the Durban Corporation in the several capacities and for the several periods of time specified below :—

Period of Service: From 11th JANUARY, 1954 to 28th JUNE, 1967.

Rank on entry into service APPRENTICE BRICKLAYER.

Promotions 15th JANUARY, 1959 – ARTISAN BRICKLAYER: 5th JANUARY, 1965 – TEMPORARY CLERK OF WORKS: 3rd MAY, 1965 – REVERTED TO ARTISAN BRICKLAYER: 1st JUNE, 1966 – SUPERVISOR (BUILDINGS AND SERVICES).

Latest Position 19th JUNE, 1967 – ARTISAN (BRICKLAYER) – SUPERVISOR'S POST REDUNDANT.

Cause of leaving RESIGNATION.

Conduct during service VERY GOOD.

Signature of Servant ;

Head of Department.
CITY ENGINEER.

Date 4th JULY, 1967.

Army Training – Love and Romance

"You will never age for me, nor fade, nor die".
Shakespeare in Love

Aubrey then undertook compulsory conscription to Military Training which included a three-month continuous camp in Potchefstroom, followed by three annual camps of three weeks duration at Bloemfontein.

Aubrey at Potchefstroom

It was when Aubrey returned from Potchefstroom, that he met Rosalie and the circumstances which led to the beginning of their future together was the result of the simple things in life which Aubrey enjoyed.

Aubrey and his brother loved to meet at the Model Dairy in Gardiner Street, Durban on a Saturday for milkshakes and parfaits.   The parfaits were deliciously moreish and certainly addictive.

Aubrey and his brother Wally at Wally's Wedding

On one such Saturday morning Aubrey met his brother, this time by accident as he had been invited to visit a co-worker on the Durban Corporation who had promised to give him a budgie, birds being another passion.   When Aubrey met his brother, they decided that they would have their usual parfait and head off to the movies and it was decided that this was a better option than going to get the budgie.

This work mate was irate with Aubrey for not turning up and on the Monday morning at work had no qualms in telling him so.   Aubrey was then sent to work with Joe Moore, Rosalie's father, who also worked on the Durban Corporation. During conversation Aubrey was invited to visit on the Sunday to have a look at his racing pigeons.   After the problem which he had had the previous Saturday he felt that he would not dare consider turning down the invitation.

Federation Homing Pigeon Winner's Cup

Joseph proudly took Aubrey through his lofts. During the tour he was told of *Queenie's* success, he was told the breeding of every bird, what they were fed, how they were trained and how many times a day they opened their bowels.

Queenie's success led to Joe's bragging rights. To win the Federation Cup, it was reckoned that this little bird had to fly about four hundred miles a day, when the sun set her wings would be tired, her body weary, her muscles would be aching. Would she fly into the night or would she roost in a tree, miles from home? Would she take a drink from a lake, a water hole or from a bank of a river teaming with predators? What was certain was that *Queenie* had raced a marathon, she had been released in an environment which was unknown, she had faced many obstacles and challenges. She had been on the win for about three days, she went on and on till she reached her home where she would ultimately drop from exhaustion. She would keep flying to win, she was an athlete; for her to win she had to beat the rest, to be the best, and she did.

The Moore family lived in Malvern at the time and Aubrey duly arrived on the Indian bus which was the only source of transport into the area at the time. Everyone enjoyed the day, and of course he became interested in more than the pigeons.

The following Saturday Rosalie was invited by Aubrey to watch him playing football. That was the beginning of a relationship which stemmed some sixty-three years.

Just when the caterpillar thought the world was ending,
she turned into a beautiful butterfly.

The engagement took place at midnight on New Year's Eve 1957. Aubrey, in front of the family and a few guests placed the ring on Rosalie's finger, promising to forever love her. It all seemed so surreal.

As Rosalie was only eighteen years old, she required the consent of her parents to marry. At first, they agreed, but then withdrew permission and it then was up to the courts to grant such permission. It took some persuading, but eventually her father agreed.

A cool windless night, the prelude to a sunny day, was when Aubrey married his sweetheart on March 23, 1957 at the young and tender age of twenty years, she was eighteen. The union of two hearts would beat as one. He had never known what love was until then. They would walk together through sixty-one years of marriage and were to enjoy many challenges, experience many adventures together and they would witness many changes in the world. He lived at a time when South Africa was governed by the Apartheid regime which enforced the strongest laws of racial discrimination. He would, however, set himself and his family free by migrating to Australia in 1970.

Group Wedding Photo: St. Joseph's Catholic Church, Greyville.

Bride and Groom: Aubrey and Rosalie

Aubrey and Rosalie on their Wedding Day 23 March 1957

Aubrey was a man who knew how to appreciate life; evident in everything he did, whether it was cruising the deep blue ocean, wining and dining with family and friends, enjoying a beer with his mates, or racing greyhounds to name but a few. Aubrey did everything with humour and style that will never be forgotten. Some of the happiest times were those spent with the grandchildren. He enjoyed every minute as he took them out into the bay in the little dinghy, teaching them to surf the wash of the bay on a surfboard and how to catch fish. In later years he had been so ill, but it was this that gave him a second chance at life.

Life never stood still for a man who had surgery for bowel cancer in June 1988, and two months later suffered a massive heart attack at the age of fifty-one years. Aubrey had a positive outlook on life and never gave up.

Together Aubrey and Rosalie had five children, Jennifer (decd), Gary, Mark, Kerry, and Susan, eleven grandchildren and eleven great grandchildren. He treated all with love and respect and was always surrounded by the love of his family and friends.

Farewell South Africa

*There are some memories that never leave your bones
Like salt in the sea, they become part of you – and
You carry them.*

*Oronsay sailing from Durban. Bernadette Urban in the
foreground.*

It was during the late 1960s, while sitting on the front veranda of their house in Montclair that the monotonous and rhythmic sound of the hand beaten African tom-tom drums could be heard in the distance. The high pitched, sustained wailing and howling of the women and dancing, common in Africa, communicating to others to gather. Ululating, the shrilling part involving the rapid movement of the tongue and uvula also inviting ancestors to come and enjoy the gathering. This always frightened the children. At the time there was mass migration from South Africa taking place to many distant lands, mainly Australia, and so like many other families, it was decided that the family would migrate "for the sake of the children" as it was inevitable that South Africa would experience major political and social problems.

First thing the next morning, application was made to the Australian Embassy and they were informed that the processing period would be approximately two years. In terms of the "White Australia" policy they had to prove that they were classified as "white" in South Africa.

The weeks and months went by as each day Aubrey and Rosalie watched and waited for the postman, a sunburnt rugged looking man, a mail laden leather bag hanging from his shoulder, as he walked down the road. Finally, the good news, the application for migration was accepted. It was then time to sell property, the house which had served as the foundation to their family life, where they had shared joy and sorrow, laughter, and tears. The essentials would be packed, goodbyes would be said and soon Aubrey and Rosalie with their four children were Australia bound.

Under a wintery sky clouds roamed freely, the harbor abuzz with boats on the waves as gulls filled the sky with beating wings and cries. The view of the Bluff headland in the distance where Aubrey had spent most of his life, where all his family had lived. It was where his Great Grandfather would ultimately settle once he was discharged from the Anglo Boer War. This day, June 9, 1970, took on a winter hue lacking the bright flashes the sun usually bestowed. Aubrey and his family were aboard the P & O ship *Oronsay,* bound for Australia, which sailed out of the harbour into a deep ocean never tiring, never missing a beat, alive with a salty breeze, and away from the bustle of life. He never forgot the vivid memories of the family and all their friends who were at the docks to wave them goodbye.

Departing Durban, they had no idea what their goodbyes would mean for family and friends who were at the docks to see them off. There were heart wrenching moments coupled with joyous chatter. The cabin soon filled with bouquets of Protea, the South African national flower, and cards from well-wishers. For Aubrey, his wife, and the children, it was the adventure of a lifetime and they were looking forward to their new life in Australia. They would never forget the vivid memories of those who were at the port, waving bon voyage.

For the next three weeks they rocked and rolled to a different sound of music each night as they cruised to the distant land. Gone were the pulsating and beating Djembe drums of African music and the concertinas strumming out the boere musiek to which they were accustomed, instead the couple danced the night away to the sounds of Tom Jones, Elvis Presley, The Seekers, the Beatles, and others.

They arrived in Sydney on June 25, 1970; it was cold and windy and on disembarkation decided to spend the day at Taronga Zoo as the train destined for Brisbane was only due to leave Sydney at six o'clock that evening. It was also their son, Mark's tenth birthday.

The day at Taronga Zoo, directly across the harbour from the Sydney Opera House was terribly wearing, the children were tired and restless. Arriving back on the mainland, it was difficult for them, as new migrants, to find the railway station. Requests for help were met with sarcasm and taunts like "speak English". They did speak English but had a different accent.

Arriving at the Sydney Central station, they were left shivering on the platform, there were a few minutes of numbing silence as they all sat huddled together on one of the benches. Soon one carriage after the other rolled into the platform which was alive with the chatter of hundreds of passengers. Finally, on boarding the train bound for Brisbane, they found their allocated four seats, two each side facing each other. There were no pillows or blankets supplied and a one-year-old, who had never slept outside of her cot was very distraught albeit that Aubrey had taken off his jacket, wrapped her in it and tried to nurse her. The two boys of ten and twelve years old lay on the floor between the seats and tried to get some sleep, while Rosalie held her three-year-old daughter on her lap. She went to the dining car sometime during the night to get Aubrey and herself a hot drink. They were so exhausted, he held her hand as she felt the warmth of reassurance that everything would be alright.

The next morning as the train travelled up through the Queensland towns to Brisbane all that they could see was dry grass and wooden houses which were built on stilts. Eventually the train arrived at South Brisbane station which seemed so antiquated in comparison to what they were used to in Durban and in South Africa. It was difficult to imagine that this was where the interstate trains arrived, and at this stage Rosalie could not help but wonder what they had done, it seemed that they had gone backwards instead of forwards. This prompted thoughts of the land, the rolling hills, the veld flowers native to South Africa, the family, parents, siblings, uncles, aunts, and friends, those who were so loyal and helpful, that were now left behind. It had become clear that migration was one of the most intense life changes that anyone could undertake.

After being met by Immigration Officials once again, as there were dozens of migrants who had travelled up from Sydney on the arduous trip; the women and the children were put on buses in extreme heat, bound for the Wacol Immigration Hostel whilst the men had to do the paperwork. Mothers were frazzled, children were screaming but the situation did not speed up the formalities. Eventually the bus departed, the trip would take another hour and once again on arrival at the hostel, the men would be called into the office to be allocated accommodation.

Finally, after a trip of seventeen hours and totally exhausted, the family were driven through the hostel grounds where migrants were let off at their allocated hut.

The setting at the Wacol Migrant Hostel was beautiful, tall Eucalyptus trees with little timber and fibro huts dotted throughout. For Mark's birthday they bought him a pink and grey galah in a cage and soon the boys were able to walk around the hostel with the parrot on their shoulders and it was talking.   The Immigration Officers visited and took photographs of this "happy family in Australia" to be blown up and made into posters for Australia House in London.

Gary and Mark

The Family at Wacol Immigration Centre

At last, the family thought that they had reached Utopia. These thoughts were short lived as they experienced the mayhem with meals served in a communal dining room with other migrants from all around the world. It was total chaos and one soon lost their appetite when the noise of six hundred children echoed throughout the dining room and one had to queue up army style to get their meals. Aubrey only attended mealtime twice, thereafter Rosalie would have to request a sick tray.

This was only the beginning as Rosalie soon found out that one of the daily chores was having to carry all the washing to the communal open laundry where the women congregated, chatted, and washed by hand. She also found that she then had to return to the hut and make the beds and mop the floors. The maid who had been employed in South Africa to do all these things, unfortunately, was still living her life in that land which they had now left behind. The children had to be taken to the communal bathrooms and toilets. This was not the adventure where the "grass was greener" which Aubrey and his family had sought so many months ago.

It did not take Aubrey long to find a job as he was a qualified bricklayer by trade and work was plentiful.

The downsides of their migration certainly began to emanate as they were only in Australia for three weeks when the news came that Aubrey's father had passed away. They agonised for weeks, was it a broken heart which they had been led to believe was the cause? The feeling of despair, the man loved so dearly, had died and they were not there to hold his hand in his final moments. Would this have been history repeating itself? Like his grandfather before him, the family were at the docks waving goodbye to Aubrey and the family; only about seventy years prior, the family would have been at Landskrona in Sweden waving goodbye to Harry as he set sail on the Brig *Galatheo*; ultimately landing in South Africa.

Aubrey and Rosalie only stayed at the Immigration Centre for about two months and then moved into a house in Goodna, which they had bought from the Queensland Housing Commission. It was here that Mark's bird would meet an untimely death. Aubrey had started training greyhounds and apparently the bird had got out of its cage when the dogs were out, and it was attacked. The next door neighbour told of the screams of the two boys as they watched in horror, Gary quite hysterical.

Kerry, their three- year- old daughter, had been ill and had picked up a school sore on the boat. Three months later, she was admitted to the Ipswich General Hospital and was under observation for five weeks. As each day passed, she became more and more frail, and it was thought that she would not survive. Only God knows how isolated and lonely her parents felt. This had certainly never been part of their dream. They now needed family, friends for support at this difficult time. This child's illness gave them a chance to rise above and conquer it, albeit that it had come at a difficult time.

Gary and Mark were then enrolled in the Goodna State School. It was not long before Rosalie was summoned to the Headmaster's office only to be told that Gary was not functioning at school, and in his opinion, Gary could not accept his new life in Australia. This dilemma had never entered their minds when plans were being made to migrate, it was accepted that the children would be better off in this so called "land of plenty". Why then would a boy of only twelve not fit into his new way of life?

Why too, when they thought that they were proficient in the English language, did they have to learn that a "vest" was a "singlet", that "supper" was "tea", that "good morning" was "g'day", that "women" and "girls" were "Sheilas" and that, a four-letter word was used to describe any and everything under the sun. Well not to worry they told themselves, they had made a commitment to make a go of their migration and they would have to accept the changes.

Other changes which had not been counted on, was that the four bedroomed fibro home which they had purchased had a little wooden outhouse in the backyard. They would soon find out that this was referred to as the "dunny" and instead of flushing one had to use sawdust to cover the deposit which one had made in the bucket. This bucket, maggots and all, was once a week removed by the garbos, and water drainage from the sink and the bathroom was by way of a long hose which ran into the garden. No one could ever have imagined the fighting and squabbles which took place between the neighbours when water from one yard ran into another not to say the least, the smell of the stagnant water which may collect and lay dormant in pools. Certainly, this was in the 1970s and times have changed in Australia. No longer do the sanitation problems as mentioned exist in most areas.

Rosalie too had not counted on the fact that when she became ill and had to undergo major surgery, she would lie on her bed and agonise knowing that her son of twelve was having to come home from school and cook the evening family meal. Her son of fourteen would be doing the washing and that

Aubrey, returning from a hard day's work would have to bath and attend to the two little girls of two and four.

Further changes occurred during the era that saw Gough Whitlam elected Prime Minister in about 1973. The *land of plenty* suddenly took a downturn. Jobs which were plentiful suddenly became as scarce as hens' teeth, and the floods which Brisbane suffered in 1974, certainly had nothing on the spiralling inflation rate. It was during this period that Rosalie found it necessary to return to work to make ends meet, with four young children and the rising cost of living she had no alternative. At times she wondered what they were doing in what appeared to be this "God forsaken land" which many years later, Paul Keating, the Prime Minister at the time referred to as "the arse end of the world".

After settling, home furnished, and the purchase of every Australian's dream, the "Kingswood", Aubrey started racing greyhounds with some success. The first dog that Aubrey had was given to him by someone who probably meant well but the dog was riddled with heartworm and no matter what he put into the dog it could not run. Reluctantly, Aubrey gave the dog away. The vet that Aubrey had taken the dog to, Graham, out of the blue telephoned Aubrey one day and offered him another dog called "Magnetic Beau". They called him "Beau" for short but when Aubrey went to pick him up discovered that he had an ulcer in his chest the size of a closed fist. With the help of Graham, Aubrey nursed the dog back to good health and in fact did quite well in racing him.

Magnetic Beau

Aubrey and his family had now been in Australia three years and had settled into their new life. He was happy in training dogs; his first major achievement was when on March 24, 1973 Magnetic Beau claimed victory in the Third Maiden Stakes of four hundred and thirty-two metres in twenty-six point two seconds at Tweed Heads. This was subsequently followed by winning another six hundred and forty-metre race at Tweed Heads on April 28, 1973. Aubrey was then well on his way to becoming a greyhound trainer.

Although everything was going well on the home front, Mark experienced a setback after he came home from school one day and told Rosalie that he had "fallen asleep while walking". She felt devastated when investigations showed that he had suffered an epileptic fit, fortunately this was a one-off episode. This was followed by a broken tendon in his hand and a broken leg. It was Kerry, who would cause the most concern, being diagnosed with Coeliac Disease, however, on the right gluten free diet she soon recovered. As the years passed, Aubrey and Rosalie often reflected on the reasons for their migration.

Once Harry had abandoned ship in Durban, what challenges and hardships would he have faced? Did Harry manage to cope with the Afrikaans language? The Enstrom family were mainly English speaking, and it can be recalled that Wally, Harry's son, working on the Railways at the Coaling Appliances on the docks, always said that he would never be promoted as he was unable to fluently speak or write the language. This would have been a major drawback.

Did he ever sit and reflect on the reasons why he had left his family in Sweden? He had left a country where those who were migrating were not wealthy and had come from the landless classes. The social conditions under which the labourers who lived or worked on the farms were sometimes exceptionally poor. In some cases where the owner and the farm labourer could not agree, life could be rather miserable and the endurance of some of these harsh conditions, was a prime factor motivating migration. Harry had adventure in his blood and at the time Sweden did not offer an outlet for his adventurous self. In South Africa he saw hope and opportunity, the seemingly inexhaustible supply of fertile land and work.

The Struggle is Part of the Story

The important thing in life is not the triumph but the
struggle.
Pierre de Coubertin

Main Street, Fernvale

Aubrey and Rosalie looked for a little property with acreage as he had planned on entering the Greyhound racing game on a fulltime basis. After months of looking for something, that was not only good value for money, but would have great potential and accessibility to transport, they settled on their little piece of dirt.

The one-hundred-year-old Queenslander situated on three hectares of land in Main Street, Fernvale about one hour's drive from Brisbane seemed the perfect escape from the city. Prior to occupation they visited the property at every opportunity. The architecture was of vernacular design, timber construction and low set. The bulk of the vertical wooden stumps, which were supposed to act as a float above the ground, had collapsed. The floor, which was also of timber construction was uneven due to the foundations which had rotted and sunk. The boys thought that they could roller skate on the floor, but Rosalie felt an expectation and prediction that these creaky, worn floorboards were waiting for someone to walk over them. The roof structure being traditional, steeply pitched, with rusted corrugated iron cladding.

The house, consisting of two bedrooms, lounge, a small passage and kitchen, was inhabitable in its present state. A little alcove tacked on to the back with windows, unpainted burnished to silver-grey by the sun and winds, must have been the pantry in its heyday; a tin chimney indicated that there may have been a coal stove in the area but now there was thick dust and withered dead creatures.

The unlined and unpainted interior showed streaks of black, aged mildew, evident where the damp had penetrated over the years, while ivy had found its way up the walls and through the gaps. The sash windows, dirty and dry with over a hundred years of grime, full of cobwebs, were in part broken and most did not open, a little tin shade on the outside extending from the top.

The cold winds howled through the patched gaps between the horizontal wooden slats, which formed the uneven walls. The front veranda ran the width of the house, the unstable wooden rails, the rickety and broken ironbark stairs dangerous. Rosalie often wondered how many boots had climbed these worn-out steps causing them to wear away into the permanent grooves. How many postmen or milkmen ever braved the derelict stairs? Geckos loved the little cottage as did the terrible looking spiders. She felt that the eerie little empty country house was feeling sad and lonely and seemed to be begging to be lived in once again. To her these old cottages were the salt of the earth which gave protection to those who had lived in that era.

After taking occupation they bought a caravan and put it in the yard near the house in which the family lived. As there was no water connected to the property, Aubrey would take two twenty-five-gallon plastic bottles to work each day and fill these and bring them home. Rosalie did the same on the weekends when she worked at the Nursing Home. They acquired an old, chipped enamel bath which was placed out at the back of the house as was an old, rusted, heavy-duty cast iron coal stove. It must have been decades since a fire had been lit in it but now, lit by safety matches, the fire blazed cheerily, the wood crackling as the large tin of water heated, on a daily basis, to be poured into the bath after dark for the family to bath under the stars.

The disused dam on the property, overgrown with Lantana bush, the half water tanks, which had obviously been used as chook pens, and an old creaky lopsided wooden outhouse, the dunny, thunderbox, very dilapidated and almost falling down, also covered with Lantana, Bougainvillea, Ivy and other creepers completed the century old scene.

Once they got themselves organised living in the caravan and partly in the house, Aubrey decided it was time to start re-building. He first renovated the old house, restumped it, and had the electricity connected. At that stage, an old electric copper urn was used to heat the water bailed into the old bath which had been moved to the alcove part of the house.

It was difficult for Aubrey as he was driving buses for the Brisbane City Council and a condition of his service was that he did shift work. He had to travel eighty miles to and from work, work twelve hour broken shifts and was away from home for about fifteen hours each day. He started off by knocking down the front veranda and steps after the postman had fallen through the gaps, so the house stood for a while without a front entrance. Seemingly their little house took on a new face like appearance from the road, the nose and two eyes staring as the traffic passed.

Aubrey, with the help of Mark fenced the yard, and managed to secure three calves whom he felt were special and named them Hilda, Annie, and Marcie after his mother-in-law and her two sisters. He also erected a rope swing on the tree at the back. It was not long after before he purchased a stallion pony.

Gary, who was not living at home, as he was apprenticed as a jockey in Hendra, and who only came home on his weekends off, bought a horse. The boys loved the free and easy lifestyle where they could take the horse on rides through the hilly terrain of the acreage.

The new house was taking shape as Aubrey built the exterior walls, surrounding the old place. He then removed one room at a time by sawing across the wooden floor and up the walls. In place of the hole, he built foundations and poured concrete to form a suspended floor, the house was transformed brick by brick. The septic tank was subsequently installed but there was still no new roof.

After Aubrey had completed building the back of the house and had the toilet and bathroom tiled and operating, it was time to get rid of the thunderbox in the back yard. Rosalie had gone to the toilet, which by that time had been partly renovated, and a snake was hanging from the rafters; her screams brought Mark running to see what was wrong and between them, with the help of a spade, managed to get the snake down and it escaped into the Lantana.

Rosalie had just returned from working night shift at the nursing home and Aubrey was ready to leave home to commence his day. Aubrey told her that he had put sawdust on the floor of the dunny and had set a match to it. It was only smouldering for several hours, so she had gone to bed to get some much- needed sleep. Gary too was home as he was on sick leave having broken his leg.

Suddenly, from a deep sleep, she was awoken to the sound of men's loud voices desperately shouting,

"Hey lady, your shithouse is burning",
and louder still;
"Lady your shithouse is burning".

She heard this a couple of times and on investigation, could not believe her eyes. The flames had transformed the wood into hot ribbons of light, sparks flying. Flickering, weaving under the spell it was sparked into, the thunderbox was like a roaring towering inferno and the men who had alerted her were the railway workers who were doing maintenance on the track on the back boundary of the property. With no town water, all Gary and Rosalie could do was stand and watch as the toilet finally fell to the ground.

Aubrey was hard at work on his days off as he, bit by bit broke down the old wooden house and, with the help of Rosalie and the children carried and laid thirty-seven thousand face bricks, on a concrete suspended floor complete with sliding aluminium windows and a green Decramastic tiled gabled roof.

Before the roof was erected, although they had all the walls, the stainless-steel kitchen sink was so bright and blinding that they were unable to wash the dishes until the sun had gone down. Having a bath resulted in a similar way as they would have to wear a hat due to the glare.

After all the work was done Aubrey decided to stop racing dogs as his original dream to build kennels on the property and become a full-time trainer was aborted. One neighbour opposed the town planning, and the building of the kennels were unable to go ahead.

Mark, however, who had helped Aubrey a lot in putting up fencing and working on the dilapidated house which stood on the land was to drop his own bombshell. He was in Grade twelve and informed his parents that he did not want to go back to school and was going to look for a job. As far as the job was concerned, he was told that if he found one, he could leave. A day or two later he came home to tell his parents that he was going to be employed as a "chainman" with Thiess Bros at Wivenhoe Dam. As they were living at Fernvale it sounded alright, so he took the job as a surveyor's assistant. Mark proved to be good in his job and in fact was taken under the wing of a German surveyor who taught him everything.

He travelled with this man to jobs at Crow's Nest, Darwin, Weipa and several other places.

Gary finally finished work with the owner of the Brisbane stables, as they thought that he had become too big, so he worked for a while with a horse trainer at Bundamba as a stable hand. The boys loved the country life and became involved in a local dairy farm where they went each morning and evening to milk the cows for extra pocket money.

Rosalie's return to South Africa

There is no place like home.

It was one of the most notable five-week holidays which Rosalie had had as it was the first time that she had returned to South Africa in eleven years. She was forty-three and this was to be the first time that she and Aubrey had been separated in the twenty-five years of marriage.

On arrival at Johannesburg at ten minutes past eight in the evening, to what was the most wonderful sight, combined with the emotions that welled up inside of her, from the air was a fairyland, and all she could think of was the song "It's good to touch the green, green grass of home" coupled with the joy of seeing a good friend, Jessie, at the airport with her son-in-law Michael. Jenny and Rosalie spent the night in Michael and Jennifer's beautiful Spanish style house and the next day boarded the spectacular world- renowned *Blue Train* bound for Cape Town.

En route to Cape Town the train stopped at Kimberley and they were able to walk to the stunning fountains erected to honour the miners, to have photos taken. The next morning, they awoke and, on looking out of the window, the sight of the rain pouring and trickling down the windows pitter pattered as they crossed the Hex River, where the vineyards and Dutch architectural houses presented the most breath taking, magnificent scenery.

The train later arrived in Cape Town, it was still raining, and although the friends desperately wanted to take the cable car up the famous Table Mountain this was not to be.

The owners of the hotel/boarding house felt sorry for their visitors because of the weather, so they took them for a drive all around the Cape Peninsula where they were able to view from the lookout, the point where the Indian and Atlantic oceans met. It was quite amazing.

The next day the friends boarded the South African Railways travel bus in Cape Town for a six- day trip through the Garden Route to Durban.

This trip took them through Paarl, Karoo, and Worcester on to the Oudtshoorn Hotel where they spent the night, after first having had lunch at the Klein Plassie Hotel, a very delightful little Dutch gabled farmhouse turned into an hotel.

Among the languages of South Africa, Afrikaans occupies a strong position in relation to English and the Bantu languages. It was, therefore, relevant that an Afrikaans Language Monument be erected on the southern slopes of the

Paarl Mountains. The monument was symbolic with meaningful features. A series of three columns to the left or west of the approach, symbolising the free-thinking west, with its advanced languages and cultures, structures which begin powerfully and resolutely and stand close together. From there they descended in a curve and then rose with an upward sweep to form the main line of the monument. A platform with three rounded shapes to the right or east of the approach, symbolising magical Africa with its languages and cultures. The inscription *"Dit is ons erns"* (This is our heritage).

The next day after leaving Oudtshoorn, located about midway between Cape Town and Port Elizabeth, they stopped at the limestone Cango Caves, declared a natural monument in 1938, the year of Rosalie's birth, and known for their stalactites. The natural beauty of the Caves was breath-taking. The word "Cango" being derived from the Bushmen – "Au-Kaum" meaning "The waters between the hills". It is these waters that have, through the centuries, carved a series of magnificent caves in the limestone bowels of the mighty Swartberg Mountain Range. Research mentions these as an infinite treasure trove of exquisite formations, delicate helictites, rimstone pools with calcite roses, stalactites and stalagmites, fluted draperies, and sequinned curtains, long slender straws, and a host of speleothems are harboured in these caves. This was a spectacular opportunity experienced and enjoyed.

The Ostrich Farm and certainly the highlight of the trip when Jenny and Rosalie decided to try their luck at riding on the back of the ostriches. They both made bad jockeys as she fell straight into the arms of an African farmhand. Lunch consisted of Ostrich liver patè, Ostrich egg with Ostrich biltong, Babootjie and vegetables and Ostrich steaks followed by ice cream and fruit salad. The local community entertained the visitors with song and dance, and all the "tickey draai" music allowing for the spinning on the spot movement.

They then passed through the beautiful Outeniqua Mountains to spend the night at the Beacon Island Hotel at Plettenberg Bay. The trip also took them on to Port Elizabeth where they spent the night at the Hotel Elizabeth. The next morning, they went on to the 1820 Settlers Memorial, Grahamstown, and East London where they spent the night at the Kennaway Hotel. The tourists then proceeded and spent the next night at the Holiday Inn at Umtata in the Transkei, then on through Ixopo, Scottburgh and afternoon tea at the Cutty Sark Hotel.

When Rosalie returned from South Africa, she was very unsettled. She wanted Aubrey to sell up at Fernvale and return to the land which they so loved. She was disillusioned with having to battle so hard to build the house in Fernvale, living in the constant mess of bricks and mortar, she had had enough.

While she was on holiday, she had looked at houses for sale on the Bluff, had contacted some of Aubrey's workmates and had got him a job back in the City Engineer's Department of the Durban Corporation. Aubrey and Rosalie discussed everything at length before deciding that it would not be the right move. For a while she was devastated. Aubrey did, however, agree to sell the property in Fernvale and move back to Ipswich.

Aubrey's Career and Achievements

Empty pockets never held anyone back.

Aubrey in Uniform

Aubrey had served his apprenticeship as a Bricklayer on the Durban Corporation and on arrival in Australia there was plenty of work in this trade. Unfortunately, it was not long before he had to give up working in the trade due to the chronic cement poisoning from which he was suffering. After much thought he applied to the Brisbane City Council to work as a Bus driver at the Toowong Depot. His service as a bus driver brought with it many commendations from patrons using the service and he became well recognised for his efforts especially when transporting children.

Unfortunately, Aubrey suffered a heart attack in June 1988 at the age of fifty-one years. According to a letter to the Brisbane City Council dated February 23, 1989 it was stated "that the Trustees, after considering advice of the AMP and the opinion of the medical practitioner nominated by them, are satisfied that you are totally and permanently disabled as that term is defined in the Trust Deed". Resignation followed.

Commendations as under:

DEPARTMENT OF TRANSPORT

JC:JE   19th November, 1981.

MEMORANDUM TO:

          Bus Driver, E. Enstrom
          Badge No. 1751,
          TOOWONG DEPOT.

          The following is a copy of a commendation received at this office on 19th November, 1981.

          "I would like to thank the driver of the School Bus on Route 726 at 3.05pm on 12th November, 1981 from Ironside State School to Long Pocket.

          My daughter aged 6 caught the wrong bus home from School and at the destination the driver realised she was upset and brought her home.

          For his kindness I would like you to pass on our thanks."

          It is indeed gratifying to receive such communications from the public.

          A copy of the above will be placed on your personal file.

Well done

                                                         B.G. Thomas
                                                  ASSISTANT TRAFFIC MANAGER

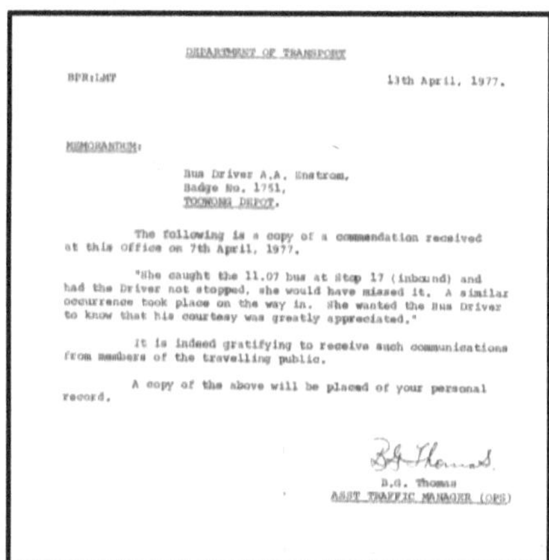

DEPARTMENT OF TRANSPORT

BPR:LMT   13th April, 1977.

MEMORANDUM:

          Bus Driver A.A. Enstrom,
          Badge No. 1751,
          TOOWONG DEPOT.

          The following is a copy of a commendation received at this office on 7th April, 1977.

          "She caught the 11.07 bus at Stop 17 (inbound) and had the Driver not stopped, she would have missed it. A similar occurrence took place on the way in. She wanted the Bus Driver to know that his courtesy was greatly appreciated."

          It is indeed gratifying to receive such communications from members of the travelling public.

          A copy of the above will be placed of your personal record.

                                                         B.G. Thomas
                                                  ASST TRAFFIC MANAGER (OPS)

Not only did Aubrey receive many commendations. Without any formal education or training he became

Director of the Brisbane City Council Employees Credit Union, a position which he held until he had to retire due to ill health.

Aubrey in the team that won the Malayan Cup in 2003 at United Services Bowls Club

He undertook studies at the T.A.F.E. College at South Brisbane where he obtained Certificates in both Coastal and Celestial Navigation as well as an "Operator's Certificate of Proficiency in Radiotelephony".

Transport and Communications
Certificate No. Q22979

RESTRICTED OPERATOR'S CERTIFICATE OF PROFICIENCY IN RADIOTELEPHONY

THIS IS TO CERTIFY THAT

Aubrey Allen ENSTROM

has satisfied the Minister for Transport and Communications that he/she has:

a) a practical knowledge of the working and adjustment of such type or types of radiotelephone installation as is, or are, specified by the Secretary;

b) ability to send and receive correctly messages by radiotelephone;

c) a knowledge of the regulations for the time being in force under the Telecommunication Convention relating to the exchange of radiotelephone communications, to interference and to the Distress, Urgency, Alarm and Safety Signals; and

d) a knowledge of the precautions necessary for the safety of the installation referred to in (a) above.

The holder of this certificate is deemed to be qualified to operate a Coast Station Class A, Limited Coast Station, Marine Rescue Station, Mobile Station and Ship Station Class B.

DESCRIPTION OF HOLDER (DOC 105A Revised Jun 88)

Height 164 cm

Distinguishing Features Nil

Date of Birth 8 January 1937

Place of Birth Durban, South Africa

SIGNATURE OF HOLDER

Delegate of the Minister for Transport and Communications

Date of Issue
16 / 2 / 89

This certificate is of use only to the person in whose name it is issued. If it falls into the possession of any other person, it should please be forwarded to:

The Assistant Secretary
Radiocommunications Operations Branch
Department of Transport and Communications
GPO Box 594
Canberra ACT 2601
Australia

ANNEXURE I.C. 38.
[Regulation 9 (2).]
INDUSTRIAL CONCILIATION ACT, 1956.

Certificate of Registration of Employer in terms of Section *Fifty-nine* (2).

I hereby certify in terms of section *fifty-nine* (2) of the Industrial Conciliation Act, 1956, that

A.A. ENSTROM,

22 ST. CLAIR CRESCENT,

MONTCLAIR,

DURBAN.

(Name and address of employer— if the employer has branches, insert head office address)

carrying on business under the style of

A.A. ENSTROM — BUILDING CONTRACTOR

has been registered as an employer in the

BUILDING INDUSTRY : DURBAN

(Undertaking, industry, trade or occupation)

in the Ministerial districts of Durban, Firetown and Inanda.

[Area(s)]

Number of certificate 10126

Place

Date 19

DEPARTMENT OF LABOUR
DIVISIONAL INSPECTOR
AFDELINGSINSPEKTEUR
14 -7- 1967
BOX-BUS 940, DURBAN

Divisional Inspector, Department of Labour.

NOTE.—In the event of sequestration, winding up, abandonment of business, transfer, commencement of additional business or change in the class of business, address, ownership or management, such change must be notified on the prescribed form (I.C. 37) to the Divisional Inspector, Department of Labour, within fourteen days, in terms of section *fifty-nine* (1) (b) of the Act and this

Certificate of Registration of a Building Contractor in Durban

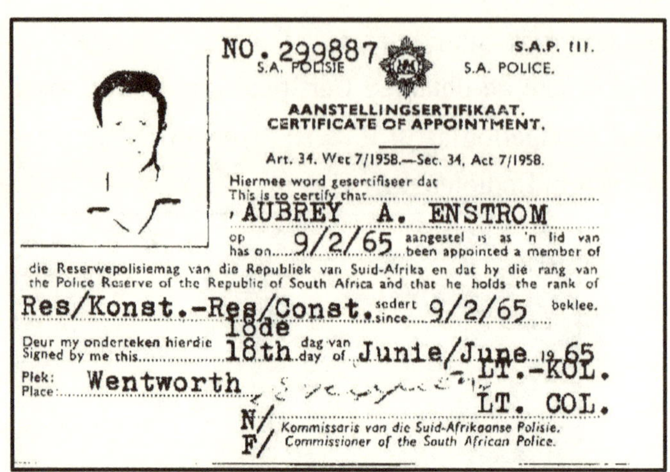

Certificate of Appointment as Police Reservist –

Durban 1965

Aubrey was very well respected and loved by his colleagues and friends and the news of his Myocardial Infarction (Heart Attack) at fifty years old was received with disbelief and sorrow by all. This was once again history repeating itself as his Grandfather too had died from a Myocardial Infarction at age fifty-nine.

Aubrey the Sailor

Aubrey on board The Silent Knight at Burrum Heads

Aubrey knew how to appreciate life, evident in everything he did, whether it was cruising the deep blue ocean, wining and dining with family and friends, enjoying a beer with his mates, or racing greyhounds to name but a few. He relished the sea, the sun, the cry of birds as he sat on the deck of *The Silent Knight*. He enjoyed the cold spray of the sea onto the deck as the boat danced over the white crested waves under the low cloud. He did everything with humour and style. Some of the happiest times were spent living on Macleay Island where he enjoyed the waters of Moreton Bay where sky and water fused into a blue palette. The enjoyment which he got from taking the grandchildren out into the bay in the little dinghy, dropping and collecting crab pots; teaching them to surf the wash of the currents on a surfboard and how to catch fish. He had been so ill, but this move was what he called life, real life.

It was in the early 1980's when he started building a yacht which he planned on sailing around the world when he retired, however, due to his ill health this plan had to be aborted but it did not stop him from buying a completed yacht and cruising the east coast of Australia.

Aubrey would become a proficient sailor as he cruised the deep and sometimes dangerous blue seas. The world circumnavigation which he desperately wanted to do, now would remain only a dream. On reflection, he had amazing determination which enabled him to cope with the complexities of raging and mountainous waves and a sense of peace and contentment to celebrate a kinder nature, the absolute calm of the oceans and dolphins swimming along *The Silent Knight* up and down the coast.

Life never stood still for a man who had surgery for bowel cancer in June 1988 and two months later suffered a massive heart attack at the age of fifty-one years. Aubrey had a positive outlook on life and never gave up. Some of the happiest times were spent living on Macleay Island where he enjoyed the waters of Moreton Bay, and the abundance of birds and wildlife. The dolphins that were always there – such a welcome.

Aubrey always reflected on the days that he was on board *The Silent Knight*. He loved to take others on board to enjoy what he had enjoyed and one such occasion he loved to see the look on the faces of a couple who were holidaying at Great Keppel Island. The calm winter's afternoon was recorded in the logbook reading;

"Left our anchorage in front of the resort beach with a couple from Melbourne and did a trip around Middle Island to Svendsens Beach and returned".

George and Shirley frequently swam around the anchored boat in front of the island. Aubrey invited them on board and after discussion it was decided that they would be accorded a sail around the island. This pair, in their late seventies, were overjoyed and were like a couple of kids on their first adventure as they did a trip around Middle Island to Svendsen's Beach, the pristine, secluded beach area on the quiet eastern side of the island. Aubrey dropped the anchor to enable them to make the most of what was available. They were totally overwhelmed with the rocks at Svendsen's Beach covered in oysters. They sat on deck and relished the dreamy seas' unmatched rhythmic pulse. They took in and visualised its glorious vastness.

After having morning tea of fresh scones, baked in the gimballed oven and jam, it was time to up anchor. On the return, there was an immediate change in the weather. The sky was darkening and threatening; the dense mist thickened and obscured vision. The skipper, Aubrey, struggled to bring the vessel around Middle Island to anchor in the front of Keppel Island. George and Shirley could not believe the change. They became anxious but Aubrey assured them that they were in good hands. Not long after securely anchoring in front of Great Keppel Resort, and offloading the visitors, a shipping warning was sounded. In very rough conditions, high seas and strengthened sea surges, he once again up anchored and moved to the southern side of Great Keppel Island, anchoring in relative calm, where waves unbelievably crawled gently to the shore and gradually drenched the sand.

The evening was spent being entertained on board *Strictly Business,* a few drinks and spinning many yarns, John informing them of the local knowledge which was so important in this area. Aubrey and Rosalie had no sooner returned to *The Silent Knight* for the night, when the emergency call was received from John:

"Don't waste any time, up anchor and follow me".

The strong winds had changed direction and it was imperative that they now move to the northern side of the island, so in total gloomy darkness, and in convoy, all the yachts which were anchored on the south side moved. It was chaotic, and calamitous. In the mayhem with the wild wind raging, and the high seas which ensued, *The Silent Knight* ended up going aground on the rocks off Middle Island as they were trying to pass through the channel between Keppel Island and Middle Island. The angry waves crashed against the boat. Boats that were following were incredibly close to the stern.

"This is going to be catastrophic" yelled Aubrey above the noise.

Suddenly, as if by Divine intervention, and with a rising tide, the vessel lifted off the rocks and they were soon on their way again. Aubrey then anchored off the northern side of Keppel Island, the only damage sustained was his dented ego. In relaying the message to the Coast Guard, John advised that "it was nothing which a couple of rums couldn't fix".

Aubrey's fascination with the sea was inbred to some extent. His Grandfather, Harry Enstrom was born in 1873 and came from a long line of soldiers who had served the crown in war and peace for well over 200 years, however, he yearned to travel from an extremely young age.

In 1889 he enrolled as a deck boy receiving a wage of twelve crowns per month. He travelled the high seas on the Brig *Galatheo*, a two square rigged masted vessel which was not only used as a small war ship, but also as a standard cargo ship.

Harry gradually progressed and in 1893 he was enrolled as a seaman, at a salary of forty crowns per month, working on the whaling vessels in the Arctic and an area which expanded well into the Indian and Pacific Oceans and it was in 1899, that he abandoned ship after docking in Durban harbour, after having experienced and loved the subtropical climate of the Indian Ocean.

For Rosalie and Aubrey, however, it was not unusual for them to park their car in front of the Royal Yacht Club, situated in the Yacht Mole on the Esplanade in Durban overlooking the Marina and the harbour. It was on rainy and miserable days that they frequented the yacht club, as they sat and read the newspapers and watched the boats coming and going. Aubrey always dreamed of owning a boat, but this dream never materialised until many years later.

He did, however, find out that his uncle owned a little rowing boat, paint flaking and showing the colours of yesteryear, which he sunk on one of the sand banks in Durban Harbour. Aubrey knew where and how to locate the boat, bail the water out with a bucket, and row around the bay fishing in certain spots. Rosalie recalled the time that they took Maureen and some friends for a day out and they were fishing. One of the girls pulled up an eel, the fear of encountering this long, slimy sea creature and having it in the boat caused a near catastrophe as she almost stepped overboard. Aubrey was forced to grapple with the fishing line and eel as he also grabbed her.

This was not the boat he dreamed of as what he always talked about was buying a yacht and circumnavigating the world when they retired. After migrating to Australia, the years went by as Aubrey and Rosalie visited every marina and boat sales office but never found what they wanted. Rosalie had sourced a marine outlet where they then bought plans and decided that they would build their own boat, the way they wanted it.

Aubrey soon put his hand to carpentry as he cut the timbers, screwed, nailed, and bent the pieces to form the framework which would form the shape. The structure seemed enormous as it started to take shape in the back yard.

Aubrey and George hard at work

George Castle and the neighbour – the Foremen

The elderly men in the area came along and took up a pew on an old drum and sat and talked of the day that the boat would take to the water, they had never built a boat before, but they sure knew how to supervise. The structure needed strength and fibreglass provided this, firstly they cut sheets of foam which was stitched to the wooden frame.

Helen and Rosalie mixed hundreds of buckets of fibreglass powder with epoxy which Aubrey, Mark and Gary painted over the woven roving and chop strand matting, layer upon layer. After much hard work the hull of a Robert's "Spray", the one like that used by Joshua Slocom when he circumnavigated the world, was completed.

● Susan and Gary Enstrom study the plans for the boat their parents will sale around the world.

Backyard boat

By SARA HEATON

A WEST Ipswich family plan to spend their spare time in the next four years building a 12m boat in their Keogh Street backyard.

The two-masted boat will be a retirement home for Rose and Aubrey Enstrom who plan to sail it around the world.

For Rose, a residential care worker attached to the Challinor Centre, and Aubrey, a bus driver, it will be the fulfillment of a 30-year dream.

The couple have visited boat moorings for the past two years looking for an affordable boat.

"For the last 30 years we have been visiting boat yards and saying 'we wish we had one' but with the children growing up we couldn't think of it," said Rose.

"Over the last two years we have visited all up and down the coast looking for a boat. We must know every boat from Coffs Harbour north, but at about $170,000 we couldn't afford one."

The Enstroms contacted boat designer Bruce Roberts and discovered they could build a "spray" boat for a third less.

For the past three months the Enstrom family have been working on the spray every spare moment. It is already taking shape.

Rose and Aubrey's four children, Gary, 28, Mark, 26, Kerry, 20, and Susan, 18, and Mark's father-in-law, George Castle, are all involved in the project.

Son Gary said their parents had taken to boating late in life, but his father had always wanted a boat.

"Dad has always wanted a boat like this. It will sleep nine and have a shower, toilet and kitchen when it's finished."

He said the boat was expected to take three to four years to build. The hull will take four layers of fibreglass and matting to the waterline, and five layers for the bottom.

"Fibreglassing should start in September. It will be 90 per cent of the work.

"Once we get it to lock-up stage we will put it on the water and fit it out from there."

Materials for the boat are estimated to cost $40,000 to $60,000, but with labour the finished product would be worth $190,000.

Aubrey was then diagnosed with bowel cancer, the trauma, the questions, the complicated surgery that would ensue. Having a colostomy would categorically not fit into his lifestyle.

He was a shattered man, the family heart broken, his dream now gone.

Two months later Aubrey felt better, the successful surgery resulted in no bag, he was frail, but he was hitting back, so it was back to the grindstone, but not for long as he suffered a massive heart attack. The game was over, so he thought. Aubrey's ill health had set him back tremendously and his dream came to a sudden end, but not for long.

He sold the hull of the "Spray" as he was unable to complete the work, and bought a steel 40 ft yacht, a John Pugh "Moonwind" design. It was named *The Silent Knight*. The hull of the Spray was sold to a young gentleman who transported it to Hamilton Island, where he intended to complete the boat.

Aubrey and Rosalie took delivery of *The Silent Knight* from Worldwide Yacht brokers at Redcliffe on March 13, 1989. That night, while still at Redcliffe, the champagne flowed and friends, some of whom were fishermen that they had met at Morris Marina at Hemmant while Aubrey was recovering, brought buckets of prawns for the launching. There was much laughter, chatter and tales to tell. The encouragement that they gave was what Aubrey needed. This was the beginning of many happy and memorable years as they lived on board and cruised the east coast of Queensland.

The next day they left the Marina at Redcliffe, accompanied by Margaret and Arthur, who had come to assist as Aubrey was not very well. The water was calm with soft winds, the waves merely snoozing and the sluggish mesmeric beauty of its beat, heart swelling, so they had to motor sail much of the way. Maybe it was nerves, but all seemed a bit squirmish; maybe it was too many prawns. Their little island in the sun, chugged along across Moreton Bay. The four on board watching for the shipping markers while Arthur told tales of his days when he worked on the rescue lifeboats in England.

Margaret and Rosalie went through what duties would need to be allocated, the type of meals that would be served, sleeping arrangements when they had guests on board and stocking the galley with suitable supplies. Eventually, Aubrey, faultlessly moored the boat at Morris Marina, in Doboy Creek, and they spent a few days familiarising themselves with everything that opened and closed.

Soon it was time to take Aubrey's "pride and joy" out for a test sail. Aubrey yelled;

"All aboard" as Lola and Eric, South Africans, living at the caravan park and who had done a circumnavigation, loaded their luggage.

Russell Island was the destination. Once anchored in Canaipa Passage, under the warm silvery sky, it was time to do some fishing. After baiting up the hook, the patience, nibble on the bait, then a tug, Aubrey shouted;

"the fish are biting", waiting, then "I have got it".

He pulled up the line and up came a flapping tail;

"it's flathead for lunch". The crab pot was pulled up next and the beautiful, massive crab was trying to escape from the basket.

Four hungry fishermen devoured a perfectly grilled flathead and crab on a bed of watercress; homemade seafood dressing added an irresistable bouquet. Lola sucked the crab legs totally clean and dry. After resting for a while, watching the cats' paws rippling in the breeze, listening to the sea lap gently against the hull, and spending a couple of days at Russell Island it was time to hoist the sails and depart. The wind had picked up, the still waters had become choppy. The crew took it in their stride as angry waves crashed against the hull; *The Silent Knight* pitched and rolled. A few days moored in Doboy Creek at Hemmant, sails folded, and they would be off again sometime soon. Their home became where the heart was and where anchor was down.

Tangalooma was beckoning, *The Silent Knight* once again outbound; the barometer was falling. They had several of Kerry's friends on board, but the weather was so rough they abandoned the trip and decided to seek shelter. They anchored off Bishop Island and although it was rough, it was quite comfortable. One young man was so seasick, he had turned "green" as he hugged the bucket, fraught with anxiety. His first attempt at sailing doomed, the weekend was ruined. Early the next morning, it was time to up anchor and return to the mooring at Hemmant. On their way back, they rescued two people in a dinghy who had engine trouble and towed their dinghy back to Brisbane for them.

It was time to attend to the compass on the yacht as it was not giving a true bearing, so a retired seaman from Wynnum was engaged to do the calibration. This was quite a stressful exercise.

Aubrey stayed on the boat preparing it for departure while Rosalie drove out to Wynnum to pick him up. He was rather elderly, and she watched as he limped toward her with a stiff leg which proved difficult getting the gentleman into the small car. A further challenge trying to get him into the dinghy to row him across to *The Silent Knight* which was moored in the middle of Doboy Creek. The calibration took hours up and down the Brisbane River, at the hottest time of the day, taking fixes at multiple points, then it was time to put Charles ashore.

Finally, after a few days, the trip to Tangalooma was made. After a cool windless night, the prelude to a scorching day they threw off the bowlines from the bollards at Morris Marina. The sun was shining, it was hot, but the winds blew cold as *The Silent Knight,* sails crinkling and crackling as they unfolded, sailed across Moreton Bay to the waters, so crystal clear, behind the wrecks at Tangalooma. These wrecks were home to the most amazing collection of fish. Dolphins provided a close up, and personal experience.

Anchored behind the wrecks, the calm sea and sheltered anchorage was magical at night, little flying fish glistening in the moonlight. The cocktails on deck and soft Polynesian music set the scene for the perfect evening, the serenity only ruptured by the raucous cry of a gull. A few days were spent behind the wrecks, enjoying the company of other yachtsmen. There were those from Canada and other destinations, the time spent some of the best that life could offer. Aubrey and Rosalie felt refreshed, relaxed, and reluctantly had to return to base.

After practising their skills around the bay, it was time for Aubrey and Rosalie to head north. Their fellow yachtsmen and friends gathered at Doboy Creek to wave them goodbye with wishes of a safe trip extended. They had a trouble free and most enjoyable trip to Bribie Island, the tides, and the wind kind to them. They took their navigational fixes and were spot on. They dropped the anchor in Pumicestone Passage, Bribie Island, and battened down the hatches. They were convinced that this cruising was easy; it was going to be the start of an adventure of a lifetime.

They call it "Murphy's Law", if it can happen it will. Aubrey and Rosalie had gone ashore with their little fox terrier, Penny, at Bribie Island, bought fish and chips, had supper and retired early for the night as they had planned on an early start the next day. At about 8.00 p.m. strong winds started blowing and howling through the wire stays, they were to experience the first real challenge of danger and hardship. They knew it was going to be rough and before they knew it, the anger in the unforgiving wind, had blown *The Silent Knight* ashore at Bongaree.

They had been to the Technical College at South Brisbane where they had obtained Certificates in both Coastal and Celestial Navigation as well as their Operator's Certificates of Proficiency in Radiotelephony. They thought that they knew it all, but nothing could have prepared them for this. What they did not know was that the anchor would not hold on the pumice stones. Why did they not realise that this was "Pumicestone" Passage?

The Coast Guard were radioed, who were more than helpful. They knew that Aubrey had suffered a heart attack only six months before, but not before they had provided him with a shovel to try to dig a trench in order that they may be able to float the boat. Nothing worked, they had to wait three days for a tide high enough to re-float the vessel. For the three days that they sat high and dry at Bribie Island, they had become the local tourist attraction. People gathered on the banks on their deck chairs and wheelchairs and watched their every move. It was very embarrassing. The bilge keel prevented the boat from lying over which was a bonus. On the third day with the dawning of a bright sunny day and a high tide, the boat was floated and before long they were on their way, subsequently arriving at Mooloolaba and were pleased to tie up to one of the pontoons.

They eventually left Mooloolaba on what was to be their maiden voyage, expecting a wonderful sail to Tin Can Bay but nothing could have prepared them for what lay ahead; nine hours of horrendous seas where one minute they were on the top of a wave looking down into gullies about thirty to forty feet deep, and the next minute they were down in the gully looking up at mountainous waves, moments of absolute terror.

The winds seemed to be getting stronger and choppier which morphed into mountains of angry waves getting higher. *The Silent Knight* took it in her stride and ploughed along relentlessly, but the crew did not fare well, and felt like throwing in the towel, but where to then, they just had to keep going. Rosalie began to wonder what they were doing out in the sea under these horrendous conditions. Were they totally mad? Finally arriving at Double Island Point in dangerous seas with cross currents and strong winds, they questioned themselves over, and over again.

Were they out of their minds? Crazy? What did they let themselves into?" As it was getting late, they decided to anchor at Rainbow Beach; although it was rough, the all-night rolling of the boat, being tossed from side to side, it still felt like Utopia after the turbulent and unforgiving anger in the sea which they had just experienced.

The next morning after anchoring for the night at Rainbow Beach they attempted to cross the Wide Bay Bar which was extremely treacherous, visibility was bad, and they could not pick up the Inskip navigational leads to take them into the shelter of the bay. The treacherous bar made it difficult for Rosalie to take the helm; she felt as though her arms were being pulled out of their sockets. All that they could hear was the roaring of the waves crashing against the hull. Aubrey was beginning to feel uneasy about the crossing, so they reluctantly called the Coast Guard for help. They were instructed to turn around and go back out into deeper water and wait. Two hours later the Coast Guard arrived and escorted them into the smooth waters of Tin Can Bay and, finally they anchored at the Marina. Sixty dollars well spent.

Aubrey and Rosalie spent a few days in the idyllic Tin Can Bay, a delightful little place, situated at the Southern end of Fraser Island, where recreational fishermen and holiday makers frequented; where the seagulls cried and swooped for unwanted fish. They needed this relaxing time to get over their ordeal and talking to all the fellow yachtsmen and locals. They were to learn that the previous day another yacht had been in difficulties and had called the Coast Guard. Whilst under tow across the bar, the rope had given way resulting in much damage to the vessel and this was now on the hardstand at the marina requiring major repair work. They reflected on their own trip across the bar and were thankful for the successful outcome.

At that time Susan was staying at Hervey Bay and she and Jack came down to Tin Can Bay to accompany her parents to

Hervey Bay. Susan took it upon herself to update the logbook. "10.00 a.m. passing Carlo Island, 2 – 3 knots, Jack fishing, dad sitting in the sun, Penny sleeping". After the moments of terror a few days prior, these were moments of sheer peace, tranquillity, and calm waters.

On arrival at Gary's anchorage in the Sandy Straits, the boat was anchored and all on board had a beautiful peaceful evening in the fantastically sheltered anchorage with birds singing in the nearby trees on Fraser Island. Sundowners were a definite as dusk gathered, and a quiet came over the Island, the gentle movement of the yacht lulling everyone into a deep sleep.

The next day they headed for Urangan, visibility was exceptionally poor, but Jack was able to spot the navigation buoys. Aubrey nicknamed him "eagle eyes".

Eventually, they were standing on the deck of *The Silent Knight* with rods in the water, suddenly they caught a glimpse of thrilling action invading the serenely peaceful waterways. No one could have believed what they were about to live through. It was in Hervey Bay that they were privileged to live through, sense, feel, witness, and experience the greatest live show on earth. The genre, a site-specific performance; the characters, the mighty humpback whales who migrated annually from the Antarctic, north to Hervey Bay.

The true to life grace and style of the fifty-foot whales provided much pleasure in a natural display of high, lively, and dynamic acrobatics as they leapt, twisted, and splashed their way onto the gigantic stage. These giants of the ocean went on a fun, water blending roller-coaster ride, breaching, and plunging their tails. The mothers caring for their young and the song of the males filling the air, captivating the audience of family and friends wining and dining on the deck of *The Silent Knight*. They provided much joy and elation in the songs from their performing repertoire. At times there were the growls, the wailing moans, which almost brought tears to all as they had never been exposed to this.

The venue provided ease of movement in their salt-water world where, these giant creatures could effortlessly move with such complete grace, providing an awe-inspiring and educational experience as they frolicked, jumping high. How totally amazing was it that they too were savouring the same fresh air and sun just as those on board were.

Everyone on board were in awe as they saw the outstanding ethereal and artistic elements of visual imagery in this playground; the lighting, sound, music composition and audio overwhelming. These creatures from the deep provided no programme, their performance acted in an unrehearsed manner, however, the suspense and thrill needed no introduction. The backdrop, the deep blue ocean as far as the eye could see. This display was pure magic. How could these amazing creatures have been the victims of slaughter in early days?

Aubrey and Rosalie then progressed on to Burrum Heads. Logbook reads "very safe anchorage, strongly recommended for future stops" and the trip was by far the best sail since starting off. They left the jetty at Hervey Bay and as the wind caught the sails, rising higher and higher, the tempo likened to a symphony, the glistening reflection blinded the skipper, as they watched the bow slicing through the water on their way to this unique fishing village, navigating through the sand flats, channels, and mangrove lined waterways. They dropped anchor and enjoyed the peace and serenity as time stood still. They relaxed and relished the mangroves, the beautiful ocean, marvelled at the above-sea world, as they looked up during the day and savoured the many beautiful sights. The enormous bright blue sky, the puffs of cloud which looked like cotton candy, the red sunset over a skyline and by night the stars that flickered like little candles. They marvelled at the many beautiful sights on offer above and below the water too. This was where the ocean ended and another world with its own beauty began.

They used the excellent facilities of the caravan park and availed themselves of hot showers and getting the laundry done at the caravan park. After a few days of rest at Burrum Heads, they were once again outbound with the intention of returning to Hervey Bay.

Aubrey went up on the deck to pull the anchor up, Rosalie was in the wheelhouse steering to keep the boat off the sandbanks. Suddenly, Aubrey became very white and went limp, he had the anchor halfway up; he called out to her but she could not leave the wheelhouse and was faced with a terrible dilemma. Fortunately, two fishermen came past, and she was able to hail them. They came aboard, one took over the wheelhouse while the other re-anchored the boat. Rosalie attended to Aubrey, his breathlessness and dizzy spells all associated with his heart failure. After a couple of hours, when he felt well again, they took off back to Hervey Bay and, although the sea was rough, it was a constant challenge but manageable.

Engine trouble prevented them leaving Hervey Bay again for a few days as they had to have the engine mounts replaced. They stayed around the Great Sandy Straits and Gary's Anchorage where Rosalie baked bread in the gimballed stainless-steel oven. It was such a lovely homely and comforting smell wafting through the anchorage.

It was decided to return to Brisbane to seek shelter during the cyclone season. John, their brother-in-law met Rosalie and Aubrey in Tin Can Bay as he wished to sail back to Brisbane on their first overnight trip. They crossed the dangerous Wide Bay Bar with ease but unfortunately followed another yacht for several miles down to Mooloolaba. Sailing the seas again provided a real challenge, adrenaline pumping, and fear as they realised that they were well off course. This was another lesson to be learnt. When Rosalie checked the navigational points, the course that they were heading was certainly not the course that they should have been taking. It became evident that the yacht that they were following was not on course for Mooloolaba; they were sailing the wrong journey. Rosalie immediately calculated another course and set a new heading – what was now needed was not *The Silent Knight's* reliability but the skilful navigation and sailing of the crew to ensure a safe passage.

It was extremely dark when, suddenly, a ship's hooter was sounded. They were in the shipping channel and far too close for comfort. It was amazing how disoriented they had become. Fear set in and they did not know which way to run. John felt that he was facing the storm of his life, a mistake at sea could mean trouble, Aubrey's eyes were so sore from the sea spray which was washing over the boat. Rosalie began to doubt the new course which she had calculated, however, total panic turned to positivity when they finally arrived at Mooloolaba safe and sound.

During the months of cruising Aubrey and Rosalie enjoyed barbecues on the beach, beach walks, exploring wrecks at Tangalooma, and cruising along playing with the dolphins. The smell of fish, the ocean, soaking up the sun and listening to the cry of the seagulls; what an amazing experience and lifestyle. They spent their time sailing wherever the winds took them. In May or June, they headed north to spend the winter months anchored in places like Gary's Anchorage in the Sandy Straits, Hervey Bay, Burrum Heads, Bundaberg, Bustard Heads, The Town of 1770, Gladstone and, of course, their favourite Great Keppel Island. In October/November they headed back south usually to Mooloolaba or the Brisbane River where they could shelter during the cyclone season.

There were the days, as the small whitecaps lapped against the starboard side, and then retreated. They entertained and were entertained by yachtsmen from all walks of life as they all shared a camaraderie and friendship second to none. There were those who regularly cruised the East Coast and there were those who came in from overseas, Bundaberg and Burnett Heads being favourites for international yachtsmen where they would get their customs' clearances.

They often anchored at 1770, where Captain Cook's second landing took place. Entering on high tide was a must due to the difficult and sometimes treacherous channel and bar. Once anchored it was a sensational spot, camping grounds, a little shop and fishing was a favourite pastime. After rounding Bustard Heads and entering Pancake Creek, a sheltered little channel, between Gladstone and Bundaberg, they would go for walks ashore and enjoy the beautiful evenings with sundowners on deck. It was so serenely beautiful, at times an un-describable peace, sitting on deck till one or two in the morning with fellow yachtsmen. There were times when someone would play a guitar or sing, other times Aubrey and Rosalie would play recorded island music and just gently rock with the sway of the boat.

Whenever they visited Gladstone, they went ashore and spent a few days with good friends, Lana and Larry and left their yacht at the Gladstone Marina which offered sheltered waters and safe mooring during bad weather. With electricity on the pontoons, it was possible to vacuum the cabins, linen was washed at the laundromat and the luxury of having a hot shower was a bonus, as was the use of the barbecue facilities. Leaving Gladstone, they travelled up The Narrows which could only be navigated at high tide. They would have to wait for tides high enough to manoeuvre the craft through the sand bars. Aubrey knew that it was imperative that he adhere strictly to the tidal criteria, necessitating the precise timing and his own navigational calculations.

From Sea Hill they once decided to go up the Fitzroy River to Rockhampton. It was a difficult area to navigate which they were soon to experience. They thought that they were in the Fitzroy River but came across some overhead power lines; the chart showed that these were high enough for yachts, so they proceeded. Suddenly, the mast hit the power lines and the sparks flew. It was a terrifying experience.

They then found that they were in Raglan Creek and not the Fitzroy River. They should have taken notice of a yacht that was on the way in, the skipper who shrugged his shoulders and indicated that he too was lost. Pilotage in the area was almost non-existent.

They eventually arrived and spent some time in Rockhampton where they replaced two batteries. Finally, they bid their farewell to Rocky and Members of the Fitzroy Boat Club before heading off back to beautiful Great Keppel Island.

On one occasion they had Mark, Margaret, Melanie and Timothy on board when a swell had developed in front of the Great Keppel Resort. They moved to Long Beach but soon found this unbearable so Aubrey up anchored and entered Leeks Creek. During the dark and stormy night, the anchor pulled out due to tidal problems and Mark had to swim to re anchor the boat with the fishermen's anchor. They had also tried to secure the boat by tying ropes to the trees in the creek. It was another night of fear and anxiety as the boat heaved and tossed about.

In the middle of the night the trees broke, the boat was drifting, and they lost their dinghy which was subsequently returned the next day by a certain Peter. The scenario was to then leave Leeks Creek but the seas outside were so rough, the atmosphere damp and heavy that they had to return to the Creek with an aroma of crisp earthly moisture from the mud flats, for protection.

Aubrey and Rosalie were again heading back to Brisbane in September 1990. How could she ever forget her birthday on September 11; they were anchored in Graham's Creek near Gladstone? She always remembered having a bottle of Mateus Rose which a friend, David, had given to her. So, the birthday memory went something like David's wine, Aubrey's cooking, and Graham's Creek. This could have been the perfect combination except that she had been stung on the elbow by a bee to which she became allergic. Her arm blew up like a balloon and was so painful she could hardly move it. They had to endure a week in this creek due to cyclonic weather and by the end of that week they could have screamed; the sand flies and mosquitoes were relentless in their attack. Finally, they could take no more and they left the creek and headed back to Bundaberg after spending some time at 1770. When they departed from 1770 the weather predictions were proved to be totally wrong.

Instead of calm they endured twelve hours of thirty-five knot winds and confused seas. It was on this trip that they experienced their first "knock down" with the mast in the water. *The Silent Knight* did not let them down and regained its upright position quickly. They could not believe how terrifying the sea could be as they watched the bow cut through the chop of the waves. These were the things that no one had told them when doing their navigational courses.

Bundaberg was a beautiful City; the people were friendly, and they met some wonderful international yachtsmen. They always used the secure facilities of Midtown Marina, located in the Burnett River, not only was it close to the City but facilities included power, water and a locked gate security and it was so easy to do the shopping for any trip which was contemplated. How could they forget the local pub which had a wine cellar and where the local yachties would take their "flagons" and fill directly from the vats. Aubrey always chose the Tawny Port "purely for medicinal purposes" as he put it.

They became accustomed to eating the beautiful fresh fish, prawns, scallops which were given by the local fishermen to those who were moored in Bundaberg. It was the most wonderful lifestyle, what they would give today for some of the fresh seafood, just nothing could compare with the quality. Noel was a fisherman who was based in Bundaberg and who lived on his own on board his boat. Noel always supplied the fresh coral trout, and Rosalie did the cooking.

There were times when Aubrey was due for medical treatment, so they often left the boat in Bundaberg and returned to Brisbane on the train.

Of course, entertainment on board was par for the course. As the entertainments officer, Rosalie found it so easy to whip up a pizza or snacks in the galley and keep the food and wine flowing. It was the carefree life, no one bothered too much, time and tide only came into being when they had to up anchor or leave their mooring to venture to another spot. That was when they sailed into the unknown, caught the trade winds in their sails and ventured to destinations to explore and discover, destinations until then they had only dreamed of.

The fun and freedom continued for those years and everyone who came aboard had a wonderful time. Unfortunately, due to Aubrey's health, they had to consider selling the boat and return to terra firma. It was a massive decision, but they decided to have one more go at doing their circumnavigation although they knew it was not the brightest idea.

They had once again thrown off the bowlines, left Mooloolaba Marina, a safe harbour, and had sailed for some miles when the seas really blew up, once again they would experience a life and death challenge. Rosalie wanted Aubrey to turn around and go back, although she knew in her heart that he would not consider such a move, he was not only a seaman, but he was an Enstrom. She turned to look at a survey boat that was following, Aubrey must have seen the look on her face as this boat was rocking and rolling in the horrifically rough seas which had formed, and quite amazingly he asked whether she wanted to turn back. She did not hesitate in her reply.

When they got back to Mooloolaba, the Manager approached them with a young couple, who he informed them, wanted to buy the boat. Aubrey said that they had thought of selling it but at that time were undecided as they had decided to do another trip at least. The young couple standing on the wharf looked disappointed. They said that they had seen the boat somewhere in Brisbane and had followed it up the coast. They had decided that this was what they wanted. They had the cash; they were more than happy with the test sail and the Marine inspection and survey. Within one week, they had moved on board and sadly Aubrey and Rosalie moved off.

The Silent Knight remains the home of the couple and their cat "Seaweed" and the memories of life at sea will remain forever etched in the hearts and minds of Aubrey and Rosalie. It was maybe that they left their run too late. Retirement did not fulfil the dream which they had set out to experience. Unfortunately, ill health intervened in their plans and Aubrey always felt that he had been robbed.

What they did experience was that their sailing took them on a journey, a journey where they could explore and discover, the life and death challenges which they would have to meet. They learned that time meant nothing to the seas, they would experience the adrenaline rushes, the fear, but they would also experience the total peace and serenity; they would grow and learn as they faced the challenges of discovery and adventure. Their seamanship was based on preparation, which did not always go to plan, experience, and a commitment. They could not abandon ship every time that they encountered a storm and so they continued to face the storms of life together.

The Silent Knight never missed a beat; it was reliable, rugged, and strong during all the time that the Enstroms sailed in it. Aubrey and Rosalie sure did enjoy the happy times, the fair winds, the sailing days and their *"silent nights"*. Their footprints were left in the sand wherever they were on anchor.

The Silent Knight on anchor in Doboy Creek, Hemmant.

The Last Hoorah

Death is the price of life.

They were rough, and tough and they came from the Bluff. They were gentlemen, heroes, fishermen, seamen, soldiers, tradesmen, and family men. These were the descendants of Harry Enstrom.

On June 9, 1970 Aubrey and his family sailed per *s.s. Oronsay*, out of Durban harbour; destination Australia. He was in search of freedom and opportunity. At the time South Africa was governed by the Apartheid regime and it was inevitable that it would experience major political and social problems. He knew that he needed to provide a better life for his children.

He cruised to the distant land of Australia, however, the hardship of migrating soon became evident as he had only been gone two weeks when his beloved father passed away. Was it a broken heart as he had been led to believe?   Once the family had settled, they had enjoyed success and disappointments. He always reflected on the changes that had taken place in South Africa. The rich and varied mammal life had not changed, although the numbers of animals declined greatly during the expansion of white settlement in the eighteenth and nineteenth centuries. Today, these large animals are found mainly in wildlife reserves such as the Kruger National Park extending over 20,000 square kilometres, the national park being home to "The Big Five", various mammals and bird life.

In the 1990s, Aubrey and Rosalie returned to a country which had undergone significant changes. Due to the uprisings in black and coloured townships in 1976 and 1985, some National Party members saw that there was a need for change. A few years later Nelson Mandela who had spent some twenty-seven years imprisoned on Robben Island, became South Africa's first black African President elected in a democratic election in 1994.

Coming to grips with the changes in South Africa came relatively easy, but what was hard to accept was the magnitude of the violence, the hardship which all South Africans were experiencing in not being able to obtain employment and in some cases housing.

What was foreign to him was the mushrooming squatter camps and shanty towns which were springing up on any available land. The fact that one was too scared to walk down the street. The fact that beggars on the streets, skin bronzed, faces peeling from being sunburnt as they were unprotected to the monotonous exposure, stood day after day in the streets begging, were so plentiful. He also witnessed first-hand what the ravages of HIV was inflicting on its victims, mainly Africans, who were brought into hospital covered in sores, some hardly able to breathe and others so ill that they could not sit up.

Seventy years prior, Aubrey's Grandfather, Harry, too was looking for freedom and opportunity. Harry Enstrom, an adventurous boy of fourteen years old, left home early one morning, and on June 12, 1889, enrolled as a deck boy at the Shipping Office in Landskrona, Sweden. He would bravely roam the deep and dangerous seas of the Antarctic, the Pacific and Indian Oceans on the Brig *Galatheo* during the whale catching era.

On a beautiful spring evening in September 1899, the Brig *Galatheo*, under the command of the captain, sailed up the eastern seaboard of southern Africa, and moored overnight in the lee of the Bluff headland. Early the next morning, Harry had made up his mind that when the *Galatheo* docked in the natural harbour of Durban, he would pack his bags and abandon ship. He had endured ten years of hardship and isolation as he cruised and roamed the oceans of the world; Harry had had enough.

Finally, as the boat docked, cargo offloaded, he packed his bags and left the boat. As Harry made his way to the Harbour Hideaway in Durban, he looked forward to meeting up with seamen from the world over. It was where he met up with connections with whom he had crossed paths many times. Ships were sailing into Durban harbour, one of the major ports in Africa transporting British troops who were part of the "Imperial" Contingents, and as Harry had longed to break free from his confines, he saw the advent of the Anglo Boer War as the ideal opportunity. Harry soon found his way to the Victoria Barracks and signed as a volunteer. He ultimately, in October 1899, enlisted in the Anglo Boer War as Trooper 289, Bethunes Mounted Infantry.

Harry was involved in the skirmish which took place at Scheeper's Nek near Vryheid, on May 20, 1900. He experienced the mayhem and confusion. The orange flashes of Mauser fire and the whizzing and whining of bullets ricocheting all around him, as he lay injured in the dust, listening to the screams and yells of fellow troopers. He was wounded in action and taken Prisoner of War.

He would soon find that the physical conditions of a country so far removed from his hometown in Sweden would take its toll. When Harry first entered Durban, it was a time of hope. Settling on the Bluff one could shoot a springbok for dinner and fish were plentiful. Durban, with its warm subtropical climate and beautiful beaches was what he fell in love with.

By the age of twenty-seven, Harry had experienced and had been engaged in the dangerous and hard life of a seaman. He had been shot, taken prisoner of war, and was medically discharged from the army. He was an invalid. To his family, Harry was a legend.

In 1910 Harry, and his family had moved to the Bluff, Durban. In later years Harry's children and grandchildren told stories about the Union Whaling Station on the Bluff. Aubrey, grandson to Harry, often told that the cousins had made regular visits to the educational whaling station. The decks stained with red whale blood and the awfully bad smells hard to endure. The thought of falling off the deck into the shark infested water was graver and more than grim.

Aubrey often recalled how, as children, they went aboard the whaling vessels in dock, where the chef fed them. His greatest delight was being given a tin of condensed milk to eat. They always knew that their grandfather had been a sailor on the whaling boats but sadly had never had the pleasure of being able to talk to him or listen to all the tales which he would have been able to tell. They never knew much about their grandfather's military service.

The site of the whaling station on the Bluff is now under military control and once again the sheer size, majestic and mystic echoing cries of whales invoke a sense of wonder and awe. The whaling industry was part of Durban's history and it is pleasing that this trade has now ceased.

For Aubrey, the final curtain fell on June 7, 2018. On June 14, 2018 at the age of eighty-one years and five months, the family gathered to comfort each other in their grief and to honour the life that Aubrey had led. A life that was full of hope, happiness, laughter, and love, through good times and bad. How he led his life was an example to everyone he had met, that love was an action not just a feeling. He was always of the belief that the practice of giving of ourselves was the truest way to honour God. He was honoured for his unselfish ways as, like his Father before him, the little he had he gave to others.

The patriarch and the pioneer of the Enstrom Family in Australia was sent on his spiritual journey as he was laid to rest in the Beerwah Cemetery, surrounded by the love of his family and friends.

Aubrey's resting place was chosen where silence falls softly within the trees, with only the birds trilling their lyrical songs within the nature that abounds. The surrounding trees reaching skywards, a haven where troubles are released. The backdrop of the Glass House Mountains, capturing serene solitude and symbolising the high moments of success in life, rising to complete the landscape. Sand from Pumicestone Passage, commemorating the first journey which he undertook in *The Silent Knight,* was scattered closest to him, his Spirit would be surrounded forevermore with all the love, happiness, and wonderment he felt there as he embarked on his maiden voyage.

The reflections, the seaside aroma took the family back to the days of sailing by his side. He was a hero; he had unselfishly put his own life at risk on numerous occasions as he went to the aid of others. It was his love of animals, birds, the ocean, waves, seashells, and toes in the hot sand that grounded his soul throughout life. He was a man amongst men, tough and fearless.

Sixty-three years later, having lived on two continents, coupled with life on board a forty-foot yacht for five years cruising the east coast of Australia, Rosalie reflected on the face that she had always thought was the most good looking. She could smell the ocean, feel the gentle sway of the boat whilst on anchor in a lonely alcove, his arms around her waist on a moonlit night. She sees those blue eyes that locked with hers on the first night as they shared *that kiss,* that thick blonde hair combed into a quiff with the aid of Brylcreem.

He was no longer the young nineteen-year old with the muscular physique, a soldier who had just returned from three months' army training, however, albeit a lot older, he was still handsome. The physique had changed, the hair had thinned and had turned white, he was determined to do it his way as his hair grew longer and longer.

From soldier to husband, father, sailor, the happy tears and laughter, the kisses had continued throughout the years, first thing in the morning, last thing at night; they had become tender, sincere, the feeling, the intimacy and the warmth were still there. The same tender kisses he shared with his children, grandchildren, and great grandchildren.

Life never stood still for Aubrey, a man who had surgery for bowel cancer in June 1988 and who suffered a massive heart attack at the age of fifty-one years. He always had a positive outlook on life and never gave up, even when admitted to the Palliative Care Unit at the Redcliffe Hospital, made it quite clear that he still had ten years to live.

Rosalie thought about the heart attack which he suffered in 1988; it was beyond her capacity to grasp how lucky they were to have him survive the ordeal. There was always hope before, but now, with the revolving door of medical appointments and his deterioration, it seemed just like a tiny flicker against the wind.

God had blessed her by giving her this amazing man and a fine family but every time she now reached out with love, she was crushed with a new pain.

Their sixtieth wedding anniversary was coming up, there was so much to reflect on over the years of their marriage, so much which was still unsaid. Rosalie felt that she was drowning, the intense emotions as there was nothing more anyone could do. She had been given the greatest gift in life and now it was about to be taken from her.

The notion of any hope had become meaningless as things began to deteriorate. The bond that kept her heart beating felt so thin.

This was a man who had sixty-three years prior promised to protect her and love her till death parted them. He comforted her when they lost their first child when the grief and trauma were unsurmountable. He stood by her with confidence and courage as they faced many challenges, sailing the deep blue seas, as they had lived on two continents and had reared their four children. The hands that never tired of hard work.

He always talked about the beautiful flowers which he had grown, the birds and how he loved the sunlight, the rain and the drifting clouds. He was always able to identify things in the cloud formations. He loved how the leaves fluttered in the breeze, but now he felt a tiredness that he felt hung over him like a constant heavy cloud. Aubrey passed away on June 7, 2018 at 4.20 pm.

Rosalie reflected on the first day that she met him when she could see the sun and vast blue of the skies in his eyes, now all she could see that his eyes had been robbed of the usual warmth. She always knew that he was the one that she wanted to spend her life with. All the days of her life she spent thinking of him and at night, felt the beat of his heart as they got close, and she closed her eyes and dreamed about him. He held her when she cried, and laughed when she was happy, their hearts knew each other even in silence.

In the end death came so quickly. Suddenly she felt the loneliness, the solitude. There was no spoken goodbye, he did not want to die, his mind went haywire, the heart slowing, breathing failing. She had taken his lifeless hand, the end was near and when death came, he seemed to be at ease, took one final glance at her as he rolled over toward her, then he was gone. All that was left was a body that had been slowly drained of life. She stood at his bedside; she was numb inside. Had the anxiety burnt out? She waited for his eyelids to open, there was no movement from his lips, there was no more anguish or strain on his relaxed and unlined face as he lay there motionless. He had found himself looking into the eyes of death on so many occasions, he grappled it with all his strength, time and time again, but at that moment, it folded him in its arms – death the ultimate price of life.

The very richly woven tapestry of their love, the successes, the ups and the downs, their travels, all the pain and suffering finally ended and their lives together had become complete and was over.

Harry Enstrom, an adventurous boy of fourteen years old, left home early one morning, and on June 12, 1889, enrolled as a deck boy at the Shipping Office in Landskrona, Sweden. He would bravely roam the deep and dangerous seas of the Antarctic, the Pacific and Indian Oceans on the Brig *Galatheo* during the whale catching era.

Harry died at age fifty-nine from cardiac failure. The Patriarch and Pioneer of the Enstrom Family in South Africa was laid to rest in Stellawood Cemetery in Durban. No longer would he be able to stand on the deck of that Brig and look up into the maze of ropes and wind filled canvas overhead. He would no longer hear the noise of the breakers and the commands of the captain, feel the terrible anxiety, and fatigue or experience the days when sailors earned calloused hands and sun bronzed backs. Harry would, however, have been proud of his descendants as most of the family had become seamen in their own right, and certainly were good and well-known fishermen.

Sadly, the once beautiful City of Durban in which the Enstrom and Moore forefathers lived, had become a filthy, dirty, squatter camp and the entire Durban beachfront area in a permanent state of deterioration and neglect.

Was this the country when in the 1800s Britain was looking for a prime port where they could trade with the local tribes and where European settlement named the town Port Natal?

Returning to Australia, Aubrey could not help but think about his beloved Africa. This was the place where many of their friends and family rested in peace. It was where others were once again being left behind, the rhythm of the African music and boere musiek would be another chapter in their epic journey.

Never could they have imagined the amount of water which would flow under the bridges that have been crossed. They would return to the land Down Under, the land of plenty, where they would give their children a better life, the land which would allow free speech, where democracy ruled and where they would be able to walk the streets freely without the threat of being mugged.

Aubrey always questioned whether he had deprived their four children of their South African heritage, their grandparents and family. Only the Lord knows how he stood helplessly by and watched the tears roll every Christmas as Rosalie basted and cooked the turkey, the glazed ham, boiled the traditional pudding, and he knew how she longed to be back with family and friends. The children were too young to miss the lifestyle, but he knew that they were given a future. They were given a chance to read and write and there is no doubt that the chance which they were given, enabled the blindness to turn to light.

In the 1800's their forefathers migrated to South Africa for that better life, now the descendants of those who had forged a better life for themselves all those years ago, were once again leaving South Africa with that same goal in mind – to have a better life.

The Pioneer of the Enstrom family in South Africa lived his life dangerously and to the fullest. The war had left him a legacy of pain, suffering and sacrifice. To his family he left a legacy of bravery, fearlessness, and valour.

The Patriarch and Pioneer of the family in Australia would experience the adventurous life which his Grandfather Harry, had longed for. He would live on board a forty-foot yacht for five years cruising the east coast of Australia.

As his Grandfather before him, Aubrey would ultimately succumb to heart failure. He too would leave a legacy of moral integrity, courage, and heroism.

About the Author

The flight to freedom, unleashed her power. The reconciliations, the peace within, the lessons learned from a little bird of unmatched beauty, who unleashed her power as she conquered the perilous skies, has throughout my life been an inspiration. *Queenie's* flight to freedom has enabled me to forge my own unique approach to life; a life lived on two continents and on a forty-foot yacht cruising the seas along the East Coast of Australia.

As a child and teenager, I led a very sheltered life with a mother who ruled with a rod of iron, and a father who, albeit a decorated World War II Veteran, was an abusive and violent alcoholic. I lived at a time when South Africa was governed by the Apartheid regime who would enforce the strongest laws of racial discrimination. The socialisation entrenched would forever have affected my mentality if I had not been able to set myself free and take control of my own life.

Involved in many challenges, I would take on the legal fraternity but would lose the fight to gain custody of a sister, incarcerated as a slave, in an institution which ran the infamous Magdalene laundries. During the 1960's to the 1990's it was juggling motherhood and family with career and taking on new interests with family members which included football, fishing, sailing, and greyhound racing. I packed up my four children and, together with my husband, migrated from South Africa to Australia. Probably the most notable challenge being the enrolment at the University of Queensland, St. Lucia at the age of forty-five and at fifty graduated with a Bachelor of Arts Degree which would ultimately affect my life's trajectory. I now felt empowered.

It was in the early 1980's when my husband and I started building a yacht which we planned on sailing around the world when we retired, however, due to his ill health this plan had to be aborted but it did not stop us from cruising the east coast of Australia.

During the five years in which we lived on board the forty-foot yacht, *The Silent Knight,* I became Chief Navigator, Ship's Radio Operator, Entertainments Officer, Galley Maid, Steward, Cabin Steward and of course, the Captain's First Mate. I became a proficient sailor as we cruised the deep and sometimes dangerous blue seas. The world circumnavigation which, we desperately wanted to do, now would remain only a dream. On reflection, I did have amazing tenacity which enabled me to cope with the complexities of raging and mountainous waves coupled with a sense of joie de vivre to celebrate a kinder nature, the absolute calm of the oceans and dolphins swimming along with us up and down the coast.

Life has never stood still, and at seventy-seven years of age, I commenced further studies for my Postgraduate Master of Arts – Writing, through Swinburne University of Technology.

I have a passion for writing and, after having researched and written the exceptionally rich history of the family, *Stockholm to Durban,* (limited publication), *The Osmers Family History* (limited publication) I wrote my own autobiography: *Flight to Freedom* where I focussed on the richly woven tapestry of my life which became complete as the final curtain fell in June 2018, the loneliness and the solitude all reflected on.

Military Medical Records

Trooper 289
Bethunes Mounted Infantry

7 October 1900

Medical Records:

Department of Health and Social Security: PIN71/2512

On the 7th October 1900:

I, Harry Enstrom, Trooper in the B.M.I. hereby affirm on oath that my domicile is in Durban, Natal

Witness: G Davis: Major

Howick   7.10.1900.

Signed: H Enstrom

His Medical Report of October 7, 1900 states that he has considerable loss of power in right leg; complains of frequent dull pain in lower part of abdomen and a difficulty in mid? Treatment consisted of rest and massage over wound in right hip. The Prognoses was that he would be unfit for further service and for work for at least 4 months.

He was in the General Hospital at Howick and the proceedings of a Medical Board (7/10/00) revealed that he was 27 years old, had eleven months service as No. 289 Trooper, Enstrom H., Bethune's Mounted Infantry. Their findings "He is suffering from the effects of gunshot wounds of the chest, left shoulder and right hip and recommend his discharge as unfit for the Imperial Irregular Forces. The disability will prevent his earning a livelihood the extent of one third disability.

PROCEEDINGS OF A MEDICAL BOARD (assembled)

At: General Hospital Howick

on the: 7th October 1900

by Order of: G.O.C.L of C

for the purpose of examining and reporting upon the present state of health of No. 289 Trooper Enstrom H., B.M.I.

Age:	27
Service	11 months
PRESIDENT:	Major T Westcott R.A.M.C.
MEMBERS:	Major G Davis R.A.M.C.

The Board having assembled pursuant to order, proceed to examine the above-named Trooper and find that he is suffering from the effects of gunshot wounds of the chest, left shoulder and right hip and recommend his discharge as unfit for the Imperial Irregular Forces.

The disability will prevent his gaining a livelihood the extent of one third.

The opinion of the Board upon the questions herein is as follows:

(1) Is the Trooper fit for service at home or abroad?
No

(2) If not so fit, how long is the disability likely to continue?   six months

(3) Was the disability contracted in the Service?
Yes

(4) Was it caused by Military duty?
        Yes

(5) Was it contracted under circumstances over which he
        had no control: Yes

(6) If caused by Military duty or service, the nature of such
        duty or service to be briefly and clearly stated:
        Active Service

        Signed.   T Westcott: Major R.A.M.C. & Edward
                           Davis: Major R.A.M.C.

13 December 1900

Adm. Ba   13 December 1900   A185873

Chelsea No.   5737

Regiment: Bethune's Mounted Infantry

Name: Harry Enstrom

Rate of Pension: 18d (18 pence)12 months conditional
                           from date of ceasing to draw pay.

Dates range from 2/9/1919 to 27/3/1923

Regiment: Bethune's Mounted Infantry

No.   289

Rank: Trooper

Name: Enstrom H.

Age: 27

Service: 11 months

Disease: Gunshot wounds Rt chest; left shoulder at rt hip

History of Case: was shot on May 20 in four places;
                           wounds healed well

Present Condition: Has considerable loss of power in rt leg;
complains of frequent dull pain in lower part of abdomen with
difficulty in mid ....; ....very well.

Treatment: Rest; (unable to read)

Prognosis: Unfit for further service. Will be unfit for work
 for about 4 months.

Signed. Campbell: CMO

No. 1465: 7/10/00 – Howick

13th January 1901

MEDICAL CERTIFICATE: (ARMY BOOK 172) (To
 accompany a Man Transferred from one Hospital to
 another)

Extract from Admission and Discharge Book of

S.S.Formosa Hospital at Sea Date 13 January 1901

No. of Case: 18

Regiment or Corps: M.B.I.

Rank and Name: Enstrom: Trooper H

Age last Birthday   28

Service: 1 year 3/12

Service in the Command: Ticked (yes)

Admitted into Hospital: Ticked (yes)

Transferred: Ticked (yes)

Religion: C/E (Church of England)

Disease: G.S.W. Back

Destination on Transfer, and to what Hospital or Ship
 transferred: England

Reasons for Transfer: Came from Howick Hospital
 without T.C.

Signed.   A.T. Holt Medical Officer in Charge.

17 January 1901

Station or Troop Ship: Woolwich

Date of Arrival at Station: 17.01.01 (17 January 1901)

Discharge from Hospital: 17.5.01

Disease: Gunshot Wound Back

No. of Days in Hospital: 121

Remarks on Nature of Disease: .... some bullets are

 supposed to be lodged in the body but could not be ....

17 June 1901

Sent to Bartholomew's Hospital for further treatment

Admitted to Hospital: 17.6.01

Discharged from Hospital: 10/7/01

No. of Days in Hospital: 24

21 June 1901

On the 21st June 1901 - Detailed Medical History of an
 Invalid: Woolwich Hospital:

His age was recorded as 28 and his former Occupation:
Clerk.

His disability was Gunshot wounds Chest, Shoulder and
Buttock which disability originated on the 20th May 1900 at
Scheepers Nek when in action he received gunshot wounds.
One entered right chest below the nipple and emerged behind
one inch and a half to the left of the spine, another entered
behind the left shoulder and there is no exit wound, though x-
rays do not reveal the presence of a bullet. He was also

wounded in the right buttock and over the spine above the folds of the buttock. Whether those are two entrance wounds, or one is an exit, wound is impossible to determine. After exercise he suffers from severe abdominal pains with shooting pains down the legs and he finds great difficulty in straightening his back after he has been sitting for some time.

The disease is the result of service, attributed to exposure on duty when in action and has not been aggravated by Intemperance or Misconduct. The disability is permanent. It will prevent his earning a full livelihood to extent of half. He was X-Rayed with negative results and no operative treatment was considered advisable.

He was proposed for discharge on account of permanent unfitness for service.

Signed. T Hartigan C.S. Medical Officer in Charge of case.

Countersigned R da Costa, Major R.A.M.C. Medical

Officer in charge of Surgical Division.

24 June 1901

The opinion of the Medical Board on the 24 June 1901 concurs in the above report and recommends his discharge from the service.

Medical History:

H Enstrom

BMI Number 289

Proposed for change of Climate or Discharge by a Medical Board

Station: Woolwich

Date: 24.06.01

Disease: Gunshot wound (Chest, Shoulder and Buttock)

Results: Invalided

29 July 1901

Discharged the Service: 29 July 1901 at Shorncliffe.

Age: 28 years

Height: 5 feet 7 inches

Chest Measurement: 38 inches

Complexion: Fair

Eyes: Blue

Hair: Light brown

Trade: Clerk

Intended Place of Residence: 17 Percy Street

Tottenham Ct Rd

LONDON WC

Address whilst in England –

Wishes to return to South Africa.

On the 17th January 1901 H Enstrom acknowledge that he had received all pay, Allowances and Clothing and all just demands up to the present date.

19th June 1901:

Memorandum to District Paymaster, Home Dist.

Will you please furnish a reply to my minute of 11th instant, asking whether you have received the statement of account of No. 289 Private Enstrom, B.M.I. as the man stated he had received money from you.

Signed. J Inder, Lieutenant R.A. for Major R.C.A.

20 June 1901:

A reply was made to the letter referred to on 12th instant to the effect that no L.P.C. had been received, nor had any pension been paid.

I would, however, point out that I received Hospital Authority (No. Col Caps dd W.O. 29/3/01) authorising me to issue twenty-eight pounds being of pay at 5/- daily from 7 Oct 00 to 26 Jan. 01. the date of the man's admission to Pension, this sum I duly paid to the man.

On the 15th instant I received another letter from the man respecting medical re-examination and I informed him that he would receive due instructions from Chelsea Hospital and informed him that he was to send in at once, his Life Certificate for payment of pension but up to the present time I have not received that document. I cannot pay the pensioner without it.

Chief Paymaster Home District.

22 June 1901:

Reply Forwarded - this man was discharged from the Herbert Hospital for one month's sick? from 18th May to 17th June. He has been readmitted to Herbert Hospital. Will you please inform me if anything is known of his discharge?

Signed: J Inder Ltd.

24 June 1901

Letter dated 24 June 1901: from R.A. Regimental District Staff Office, Woolwich to Officer Commanding, 1st Provisional Bn., Shorncliffe.

With reference to Minute 3 of attached can you please say whether any steps have been taken to carry out the discharge of this man.

26 June 1901

Reply: No steps have been taken here to carry out this man's discharge. C.M. Kelly.

Letter dated 26 June 1901: to Registrar and Secretary, Herbert Hospital from Capt. Adjt. R.A. Reg District Staff.

Will you please say whether it is proposed to invalid this man?

Reply: This man is about to be invalided the service.

8 July 1901

Letter dated 8 July 1901: to Adj. R.A.D. Staff:

As this man's discharge will be carried out by 06, 1st Prov. Bn. Shorncliffe, will you please forward this correspondence to that office.

With reference to minute 2, he would appear to have been previously admitted to pension.

9th July 1901:

Forwarded for your information, this man states that he received a discharge in South Africa and that his pension papers are now with the Home District.

29 March 1903

Medical Report:

Wounds completely healed but he complains of pains in different parts of body, and it is possible that there is a bullet lodged as there is no exit aperture from his third wound in his buttock.   Patient is lame from stiffness in left hip, not permanent will improve: probable minimum duration 6 months. Average earnings during the past 12 months two pounds a week.

Present weekly earnings three pounds.

14 February 1903

Medical Report carried out in Durban.

Employment cited as De Waal and Co., Point Durban: Foreman at 10/- a day.

Report (Undated) states that his wounds remain healed, he suffers, as patient states from pains (vague) in chest which come on suddenly on any exertion, except slow walking. His heart seems to stop beating for a moment or two on such occasions. He has no lameness, the only physical sign detected is slight irregularity in the heart's action. He smokes but not to excess.   The irregular heart's action possibly permanent but will improve to a great extent.   Wounds completely healed, not equal to the loss of a limb.

If patient can get a situation like his former one of overseer of natives, his capacity for earning a livelihood is hardly impaired at all but at manual labour, his capacity would be impaired to the extent of quarter fully.

Follows the occupation of "Handyman", Carpenter, or overseer of natives.

Average weekly earnings for past 18 months about 6/- a day (but he has had no work for 5 months). He is out of work at present.

Last Employer: Messrs. De Waal and Co., Shipping Agents, The Point, Durban.

16 February 1904

Letter dated from The Director General, Army Services, 68 Victoria Street, S.W.

I am directed by the Lords and others, Commissioners of this Hospital, to transmit to you the discharge documents of the Soldier named below (No. 289 Private Harry Enstrom, B.M.I., Address c/o Chief Paymaster, Pretoria) for the reason assigned in the margin, and to request that you will be good enough to cause them to be returned with the information required.

For favour of your advice as to whether there is a permanent disability in this case, and if so, to what extent, or whether it is advisable to keep him longer on the conditional list. He was wounded nearly four years ago. Admitted to Pension 18 December 1900: Rate 15d. Expires 29.3.1904.

I have the honour to be, Sir, Your obedient Servant,

G.S. Schmiabe? Major General, Lieutenant Governor and Secretary.

17 February 1904

Letter: to Secretary, Royal Hospital, Chelsea.

It is recommended that the disability of H Enstrom, late of B.M.I. be considered to affect his earning capacity to the extent of one-fourth for a further period of twelve months.

Renewals etc. which have taken place since discharge:

17 April 1902   10/6d.   8 months conditional

26 March 1903   8/9d.   12 months conditional

25 February 1904 8/9d.   12 months conditional

23 February 1905 5/3d.   Permanent

3 May 1908

Letter written by Secretary of State, War Office, London, SW.

Addressed to the Secretary, Royal Hospital, Chelsea, SW.

I am directed to inform you that the man named in the margin (Harry Enstrom, B.M.I. at 1s 6d. adm: 13.12. 00) received pay at Shorncliffe on the strength of the 1st Provisional Battalion up to and for the 29 July 1901 and the date of commencement of pension was, therefore, post-dated to the 30th July.

As the present grant does not expire until the 29th July 1908, I am to request that you will state whether the Commissioners of Chelsea Hospital desire that instructions should be given for payment of the renewal of pension awarded by them on the 17th ultimo, (Inv.Pd. Case No. 146) or whether they consider that further medical re-examination will be necessary.

Letter undated by Harry Enstrom to Officer Commanding, Provisional Battalion, Shorncliffe:

"I hereby certify that I have not received any money on account of pension".

15 March 1920

Medical Report on an Invalid:

Date of origin of disability: 20 May 1900 –

Place of origin of disability: Scheeper's Nek.

Received multiple wounds in action as enumerated above. Has been on pension since date of discharge from the army. Now finds that his earning capacity is decreasing as a result of these wounds and has applied for increase in pension. He complains of pain when in certain positions and is unable to remain long in any one position without it causing much inconvenience which he attributes to bullets in different parts of the body. He thinks three still remain embedded in the tissues. Active service Anglo-Boer War.

General health excellent, physique - above normal, Heart and all organs appear to be unaffected. No definite symptoms present, but if the number and positions of the various wounds are taken into consideration it is highly probably that a certain degree of disablement still exists.

See X-Ray Report attached.

Signed. Durban Mar. 5th.1920 (G.D.) E.L. Wright

30 March 1920

Letter dated Durban from Sanatorium, Chelmsford Road, Durban to Military Pensions, Medical Officer, Durban.

With reference to the abovenamed, a thorough screen examination was made of the entire body, which failed to reveal any bullet or other foreign body.

The patient states that he had acute pain in the right leg for a considerable time and could distinctly feel a bullet against the bone. A Radiograph was taken of this area to reveal any bony lesion, if any. On examination, no abnormality could be detected.

Signed. L.M. Forsyth.

10 April 1920

Application for increase under Royal Warrant of 17.4.18 for former Wars dealt with under P.W.P. 2481.

Renewal or Revision of Award - Medical Board Report

Decision: Increase Pension to 5/6d. per week from 1 April 1919 to 2 September 1919 then 8/- for life.

25 September 1922

Letter dated from Ministry of Pensions to Mr H Enstrom, Late B.M.I. (289).:

In order to enable your case to be investigated, I am directed by the Minister of Pensions to request that you will be good enough to furnish the information required overleaf, fold and return this form to the address shown on the back of this form.

Signed. William Sanger: Director General of Awards.

26 March 1923

Letter from Mr Chalmers,

Kindly say whether the attached Minute to P10 should be audited and whether duplicate P7's for last award should be sent. C.I Cox.

Reply: As the current award was authorised by the Ministry, we had better ask A/C 6 to stamp, duplicate P's will not be necessary.

10 November 1923

Letter dated from Military Pensions Board, Pretoria to Ministry of Pensions:

Your letter of the 25 September 1922, No. P.W.P. 5737/C addressed to the abovenamed care of this Department is returned herewith.

Letter from Military Pensions Commissioner, Church Street, Pretoria to The Ministry of Pensions, Burton Court, King's Road, London, SW.3

I beg to furnish herewith copy of medical report of Board held on the abovenamed ex-soldier on the 15th March 1920 for your information, please. Your 2421/5737/C refers.

5 March 1926

Letter from Overseas Awards Branch to Chief Pensions Officer, The Treasury (Pensions Office), Pretoria, South Africa.

I am directed by the Minister of Pensions to request that you will forward the enclosed forms M.P.A.110 and 110.A, to the abovenamed man for completion, in order that consideration may be given to an increase of his pension under the Royal Warrant 13 March 1925: the terms (Amendment) 1924.

Mr Enstrom should be informed that the Declaration should be returned to you duly completed as early as possible, and that it is of the greatest importance that the instructions given on the forms should be strictly carried out, otherwise there may be considerable delay in giving a decision as to his eligibility for an increase of pension.

It is requested that you will be good enough to scrutinize the form before returning it to this Department and will draw the pensioner's attention to any omissions or obvious errors.

Further, I am to request that you will be good enough to state whether a Supplementary Grant is and if so, to favour this Department with full particulars.

Signed. G.C. Ricketts for the Secretary.

5 May 1926

Reply: I beg to acknowledge the receipt of your letter No. 5576/OS/M of 5 March 1926 and to forward herewith letter in original received from the abovenamed for your information.

Letter from Harry Enstrom, Fynnlands, Bluff to The Chief Pension Officer, Pretoria.

My means for the last year, has been over two hundred pounds so am not compl. form M.P.A.110 and 110A.

I am, Sir, Yours respectfully,

Harry Enstrom.

26 March 1928

Renewal or Revision of Award:

Certified that the pension charge of Twenty pounds sixteen shillings per annum has been taken over by the South African Government as from 1.4.27.